"You're quiet tonight," she said.

Doug looked at Nina as they danced. "Just thinking how happy the bride and groom look."

"They'll have a great marriage. In sickness and health—that's important."

Her words jarred him. Was Nina sick? Is that why she said marriage for her was impossible? Possibilities spiraled in his mind, but he didn't pursue them. "They'll make tremendous parents. You know, a guy at work told me that no one's prepared for parenthood. It's learn as you go."

"I've been trying to tell you you're wonderful with Kimmy. You should be a dad. You're the sweetest man I know."

He saw sadness slip across her face. "Don't you want to have a child?"

She hesitated…only a second…but he caught it. "Very much."

So why did she pause?

He had to find out. But he knew pushing her would make her put up a wall. Instead, he'd be patient.

The woman in his arms was worth waiting for.

Gail Gaymer Martin is a multi-award-winning novelist and writer of contemporary Christian fiction with fifty-five published novels and four million books sold. CBS News listed her among the four best writers in the Detroit area. Gail is a cofounder of American Christian Fiction Writers, a keynote speaker at women's events, and she presents workshops at writers' conferences. She lives in Michigan. Visit her at gailgaymermartin.com. Write to her online or at PO Box 760063, Lathrup Village, MI, 48076.

Books by Gail Gaymer Martin

Love Inspired

The Firefighter's New Family
Rescued by the Firefighter
A Mother to Love
A Husband for Christmas

Loving

Loving Treasures
Loving Hearts
Loving Ways
Loving Care
Loving Promises
Loving Feelings
Loving Tenderness

Dreams Come True

A Dad of His Own
A Family of Their Own
A Dream of His Own

Visit the Author Profile page at Harlequin.com for more titles.

A Husband for Christmas

Gail Gaymer Martin

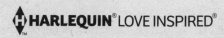

Recycling programs
for this product may
not exist in your area.

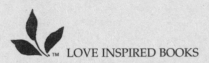 LOVE INSPIRED BOOKS

ISBN-13: 978-0-373-81866-2

A Husband for Christmas

Copyright © 2015 by Gail Gaymer Martin

All rights reserved. Except for use in any review, the reproduction
or utilization of this work in whole or in part in any form by any
electronic, mechanical or other means, now known or hereinafter
invented, including xerography, photocopying and recording, or in
any information storage or retrieval system, is forbidden without
the written permission of the editorial office, Love Inspired Books,
233 Broadway, New York, NY 10279 U.S.A.

This is a work of fiction. Names, characters, places and incidents are
either the product of the author's imagination or are used fictitiously, and
any resemblance to actual persons, living or dead, business establishments,
events or locales is entirely coincidental.

This edition published by arrangement with Love Inspired Books.

® and TM are trademarks of Love Inspired Books, used under license.
Trademarks indicated with ® are registered in the United States Patent
and Trademark Office, the Canadian Intellectual Property Office and in
other countries.

www.Harlequin.com

Printed in U.S.A.

She became his wife. Then he went to her,
And the Lord enabled her to conceive,
And she gave birth to a son.
—*Ruth* 4:13–14

Many thanks to the helpful residents and store employees who answered questions and welcomed me to Owosso, Michigan, the setting of this novel series. Much love to my husband, Bob, who supports me in this career in a multitude of loving ways. He is my inspiration for the love, joy and faith found in my novels.

Chapter One

"Why did I say yes?"

Nina Jerome looked out her front window at the neighbors toting folding tables and chairs or picnic tables for their annual end-of-summer block party. She'd tried to refuse the invitation, but her neighbor Angie Turner wouldn't listen, and Angie didn't give up.

Retracing her steps to the kitchen, she opened her refrigerator and eyed her pasta salad. It looked a bit bland so she sprinkled sliced ripe olives and slivers of red peppers on top for color. She would attend whether she wanted to or not so no one would think of her as antisocial.

She shrugged. Who would care? In the few months she'd lived on Lilac Circle, she'd gotten to know very few people, but she preferred it that way. Or did she? "Face it, Nina. You can't be a recluse. You need to meet your neighbors." She spoke aloud to herself, and then chuckled.

She had become a master of having great conversations with herself—or should she question her sanity?

The sound of the doorbell drew her from the kitchen. When she opened the door, she wasn't surprised. "Hi, Angie. I—"

"You're joining us, aren't you?" Technically it was a question, but Angie's expression was only allowing one answer.

"I sure am." She tried to brighten her voice. "I just put some finishing touches on my salad. It's ready." She opened the front door wider.

Angie stepped in. "Can I help you carry something? You don't need a table. You can share ours, but you might want a lawn chair."

Nina motioned for Angie to follow her to the kitchen. Angie carried her salad, and she grabbed a lawn chair in one hand and a plate of cookies in the other.

Angie led the way across the street and down the block. Cars lined her end of the street where they'd been moved to make space for the food tables.

Angie's soon-to-be stepdaughter, Carly, played on their front lawn with three other children. One girl, Nina suspected, was the niece of the single guy she'd heard about. It was probably that information which had discouraged her from attending the event.

When she'd first met Angie and admitted she

was divorced, Angie had mentioned the single man who was caring for his young niece. Nina sensed an ulterior motive, and any reference to matchmaking stopped her cold. She'd had enough of men. Todd had walked out of their marriage at the worst time in her life without an apology or even an attempt to offer a sensible explanation. She had to provide one for herself. And she didn't like what she'd come up with.

"You can put your food down there on the tables." Angie pointed toward a row of long tables behind the sawhorses. "We'll be eating soon."

Following Angie's direction, she worked her way around the lawn chairs, giving a nod to those she hadn't met. When she found a spot for her pasta salad and shifted items to make room for her cookies, an elderly gentleman appeared beside her. "You've made a friend today, neighbor."

She looked up and couldn't help but smile, a real smile, at the man's glinting eyes and friendly greeting.

He extended his hand. "Everyone calls me El."

"El must stand for something." She grasped his palm.

"Elwood Barnes." His eyebrows lifted. "And you are…besides being the lady who brought cookies?"

"Nina Jerome. Everyone calls me Nina." She chuckled, captured by the smile in his eyes. For the first time since she'd moved, she felt comfortable with a stranger. "I also brought a pasta salad." She pointed toward the selection of dishes. "With olives and red peppers on top."

"I'll be sure and try some." He motioned toward a man sitting alone on a lawn chair. "Come meet my neighbor across the street."

While he steered her closer, she tensed, suspecting she was about to meet the single man on the block. He was good-looking with light brown hair and one of those five o'clock shadows that gave him an attractive rugged look, yet he appeared bored, as if someone forced him to join the party. She almost chuckled, aware of the similarity to her attitude.

"Doug, this is another new neighbor, Nina." El shifted his focus. "Jerome, is it?"

Doug rose and jammed his hands into his pockets, his expression polite but stoic.

She eyed him without making a move.

"Nina, Doug Billings and little Kimmy over there." El pivoted and motioned toward the children. "They moved here a month or so before you did if my old brain recalls."

Doug glanced toward the children. "I'm sort of caring for my niece."

She pressed her lips together, hoping not to laugh. "Sort of caring?"

He shook his head, as if waking from a bad dream and finally looked at her. "I do my best."

He looked more uncomfortable than she felt.

"Nice to meet you, Doug." She detested the meaningless phrase. "I'll head back before Angie thinks I ran off. Thanks, El, for introducing yourself and for…" She motioned toward Doug. "I'm sure I'll see you both around." She strode away, monitoring her legs to keep from running.

Avoiding meeting people had become a new problem. Though never outgoing, she knew how to be civil and welcoming. And she liked El. He was a sweet grandpa-type.

"There you are." Angie looked at her, a hint of coyness in her grin.

Nina grasped her lawn chair and pulled it open. "El is a real gentleman. He introduced himself." She slipped into the chair.

"He is." She arched a brow. "Meet anyone else?"

The telltale look on Angie's face gave her away, and Nina squirmed. "You must have seen El introduce me to Doug Billings."

Angie grinned. "I wondered where you'd gone so long, and then I noticed you with him."

"He's worse than I am, Angie. Either he's very shy or he's preoccupied."

Angie shrugged. "I suppose he's worried about his sister. It has to be hard on Kimmy to be away from her mom so long. It's already been over a month. I think Doug had planned to watch her for a week or so while his sister and her friend went on a trip, and then the accident happened.

Now she can't travel or do much for herself with her injuries. Two broken legs plus he mentioned something about a torn retina."

Nina shook her head, unable to imagine what it would be like in that situation and stranded from her child.

Stranded from her child. She felt that way at times. Having a physician tell her she could never carry a child to term and, in fact, might never get pregnant again sliced through every nerve. Her husband's lack of compassion, his turning his back on her and walking away at a time she needed his love, had destroyed her trust and hope of being a wife, let alone a mother.

"Nina?"

She jerked her head upward. "Sorry. I was empathizing with Doug and his sister, I guess." She shifted her gaze, wanting to drop the topic. "The kids seem to be having tons of fun."

Angie nodded. "I hate to stop them." She motioned toward the tables. "But it's nearly time to eat." She swung back, a question in her eyes. "Did you receive your wedding invitation?"

"I did. Thank you." Envy stabbed at her heart. "Sorry. I should have mentioned it."

"No need to apologize. A cousin called a couple days ago and said hers hadn't arrived. I know I sent it so I'm a bit antsy now."

"It was most likely a fluke, Angie. Mine came

three weeks ago. I wouldn't miss the wedding. Carly's your flower girl, right?"

A glow filled Angie's face. "She is, and she'll look beautiful. I adore that little girl."

"I know you do." She swallowed. "I'm ashamed to say that sometimes I envy you."

"Why? It could be you one day, Nina. Love happens even when you least expect it, and it covers all the flaws and fears we've carried into our lives. Everything worthwhile deserves a second chance."

Angie's words sank in, and though she loved the idea, it seemed impossible. "You might be right." She scrutinized the tables overflowing with casseroles and platters. "I think you're definitely right about the food. I see people heading that way."

Angie looked again. "Then we should round up everyone, I suppose."

"Can I help?"

"I was thinking about inviting El to sit with us." Angie gestured toward his house. "Do you mind asking him?"

"Not at all." She bounded from the chair and retraced her steps toward El's front yard. As she approached, Doug crossed the street with a dish, set it on the table and approached her.

"Hi." He gave her a hangdog look. "I'm afraid I hadn't been very welcoming when Mr. Barnes introduced us." He tucked his hands into his pockets again.

Was that a nervous habit or a way of binding his hands to keep them out of mischief? She grimaced at her thought. "You're forgiven. What's in your dish?"

A faint grin curved his full lips and she spotted a different side of him emerging. "Baked beans. You know. I open a can, pour them into a casserole, add a dash of Worcestershire sauce, dice up onions and cocktail wieners and bake. It's one of my limited bachelor dishes."

Her pulse skipped, wondering how this nice-looking man escaped getting caught up in wedding bells. She often wished she'd made a wiser choice. "I don't think marriage is for everyone."

His eyes narrowed slightly until he shrugged. "Maybe, but in my case life got in the way, I suppose."

Digesting his words, she realized life had got in her way, too. "And you have Kimmy to care for. You must be a special uncle."

"Not really. Love motivates." He looked downward as if embarrassed. "Speaking of Kimmy, I hope she's at Angie's. I forgot the beans and went inside for a few minutes." He shrugged.

"She was playing ringtoss in the front yard."

He craned his neck to check for himself. "She's in good hands. When you go back would you ask her to come home? It looks about time to eat."

"Sure will." She turned toward El, noticing he had a card table sitting with two chairs on his front lawn.

El smiled as she arrived.

"Angie asked me to invite you down to her table to eat."

He gave her a wink. "Tell her thanks, but I've already made plans with Birdie. Angie'll understand."

"Birdie?"

He grinned as if she were in on a joke.

"Okay, I'll tell her. See you later." She headed back to Angie's, curious about El's sudden friendship to Birdie.

When she told Angie, her eyes widened like a full moon. "You are kidding."

"No. He said you'd understand." She anticipated an explanation, but Angie only stared at her with her mouth agape.

Finally Angie chuckled. "Birdie has been one of those neighbors everyone's tried to ignore." She released a long breath. "But you realize El has a loving heart. One day, he asked me to befriend her because he suspected part of her problem was loneliness."

"He asked you?"

"Me." Angie rolled her eyes.

"Why?"

She shrugged.

"I'm not sure since I was the one who called

her a gossip. I felt ashamed, but I did it because he asked. I baked cookies, of all things, and went to visit, but she wasn't home. I praised the Lord for the reprieve."

Nina couldn't help her chuckle. "And then what?"

"Birdie appeared at my door a couple days later saying she'd heard I'd been snooping around. When I told her why I'd come, she actually apologized in her own way, and softened a bit. She even had a bounce to her step when she left." She lifted her shoulders. "Maybe she's been thinking about her behavior and realizes she's chasing people away rather than making friends. I have no idea but something happened."

"Good for you."

"Have you met Rema?"

Nina checked the direction of Angie's gaze and spotted a woman heading their way. "No, I don't think so."

"Then it's time you two meet." Angie flagged her over. "I thought you were missing the party?"

"No, I goofed. I thought my casserole was warming in the oven." She shook her head. "But I'd forgotten to turn it on." She lifted the cover. "I hope I'm not too late."

"People have just begun to eat." Angie motioned toward Nina. "Rema, I don't think you officially met Nina Jerome."

Nina extended her hand, and then recalled

Rema was holding a heavy casserole so she let her hand drop. "I'm glad to meet you."

Angie rested her hand on Rema's shoulder. "If you have no other plans, please join us. We have lots of room here." She motioned to the picnic bench and the long table she'd butted up next to it.

"No plans. I'm just being neighborly." She gave a shrug. "Thanks for the invitation." She tilted her head toward the food. "I'd better get this to the table before everyone's eaten." She turned and hurried down the street.

Nina eyed the food line and spotted Doug standing alone in front of his house. A lonely feeling crept through her. She'd been doing the same thing since Todd had turned his back on her. Alone. Her memory kicked in, and she snapped her finger. "Doug asked me to tell Kimmy to go home so she can eat."

Angie eyed the line and then turned toward Rick. "Time to eat." She pointed down the street.

Carly bounded across the grass with Kimmy on her heels. "Can Kimmy eat with us? We have room." She gestured to the long folding table.

Angie looked down the road. "Kimmy, you need to ask your uncle Doug first. If he says yes, tell him we have plenty of room at our table and he's invited, too. I don't want him eating alone. Okay?"

Kimmy nodded, and Carly jumped in on the task.

Angie grinned. "Okay, you can both go, but wait down there. We're going to get in line, too."

"I'll go with them." Before Angie responded, Nina followed behind the children. As she neared Doug, she scrutinized him in a way she hadn't before. When they met earlier, she'd noticed his good looks but not his physique. He had to be nearly six feet with a lean waist and a great set of shoulders. She liked his executive haircut that seemed to have a mind of its own.

Doug stood as she neared, and she hoped he hadn't noticed her steady gaze. By the time she arrived, the girls had already given him the invitation.

"I'm sorry, Doug. I almost forgot to deliver your message, but here she is." She chuckled, hoping he would smile. "You might as well join us."

He hesitated, a thoughtful expression growing.

"I'm sitting with them, too. Makes it more of a party."

"Please, Uncle Doug." Kimmy's plaintive urging did the trick.

"Why not?" He shrugged, and again his hands vanished into his pockets.

Nerves or a habit? She longed to know which.

When Angie arrived, the kids joined her, and then she and Doug fell into line.

When Nina spotted Doug's baked beans, she took a big spoonful and he gave her a smile. Surprised, she grinned back, liking that he'd finally let her see a new side of him. The man was too attractive to not smile. She completed her plate with a slab of ham, but chuckled when the girls headed for the hot dogs. Kids and hot dogs.

"I'll check out desserts later." She tilted her head toward the array of goodies and maneuvered her way back to Angie's table with Doug's smile the sweetest treat of all.

Doug stared at his plate, wishing his appetite would return. He'd become overwhelmed by too many things. He'd always been a responsible person, sure of his decisions and able to roll with the punches. Not lately. He'd weighed the reasons, and the best answer he found was Roseanne's accident and feeling unprepared to be a temporary father figure. Though he could handle a multi-faceted career, he had no idea how parents kept up with a child's energy and needs. No wonder he'd hesitated looking for a wife.

He looked at Nina. Something about her captured him. Although nice looking, she wasn't a woman most men would call beautiful, yet he saw a kind of beauty. He admired her long wavy hair, the color of a chestnut, sort of brown with hints of red. She tied it back, and he longed to see it flowing around her shoulders. Her eyes tilted downward, and though she held a direct gaze, something in her eyes seemed haunting. She had an appeal that went deeper than physical beauty.

Delving his fork into pasta salad, he stopped his musing. Women hadn't penetrated his hardened mind for years, so why now? His job kept him busy, and he'd always tried to be there for his sister, whose life hadn't been the smoothest. And then sweet Kimmy. That broke his heart.

He swallowed hard, forcing the pasta down his throat and following it with a long drink of iced tea.

"You're quiet."

Nina had leaned close enough for him to smell her fragrance, like fresh-picked fruit. "Sorry." He managed a grin. "My mind got tangled somewhere. I think in your scent. You took me away to an orchard. I could almost hear birds singing." A flush grew on his cheeks. "Sorry, I got carried away."

Nina grinned. "It was a lovely compliment." She paused while a question flickered in her eyes. "What kind of birds?"

He laughed and it felt odd. "I'll have to think about that."

When she chuckled, his spirit lifted. How long had it been since he'd really laughed?

Though they had been talking drivel, his shoulders had eased, and a good feeling rolled through him. He glanced toward Kimmy to make sure she was behaving. But he had no need to worry.

She and Carly were talking and giggling like old friends. "I'm glad the girls have each other. I moved here at a terrible time. I'd thought Roseanne would be back by the time moving day arrived, but with the accident…" He shook his head.

"Kimmy seems to have adjusted well. You're, apparently, doing a good job."

"I've misled you if you think that. Every day was a struggle until Carly came along. I was trying to balance my work hours with child care hours. Can you imagine my telling her bedtime stories?"

"I can." Her grin broadened. "You have a nice speaking voice, and I'm sure you can read." She added a wink. "And, most of all, you love her. I can tell."

His cheeks warmed with her compliment. "Thanks. I do love her."

"You'll make a good dad one day."

Her comment addled him, and not knowing what to say, he changed the subject. "What brought you to Owosso?"

"I work in public relations, and I was tired of traffic and high-priced apartment rentals. I couldn't afford a house in the city. So when I learned we had a branch in Owosso, and I could transfer, I jumped at the chance. Home prices are much better here. Payments are less than my apartment."

"I found that to be true, too. But do you like small town living?"

"I've only been here a few weeks, but I think I do. It's friendly. Have you ever had a block party in downtown Chicago? Or Detroit?"

He chuckled, but before he responded, Angie's voice cut through their prattle.

"What are you two laughing about?"

"The weather." Nina grinned. "About apartments in the city versus owning a home out here."

Angie's fiancé, Rick, nodded. "I'm with you on that one. Not so much the price but the space and freedom. Carly loves the yard. My apartment doesn't have one."

Angie rose. "Anyone ready for refills?"

Rick eyed the girls. "More food, ladies, or dessert?"

Kimmy bounced beside him. "Me, too, Uncle Doug?"

After he gave her permission, Angie and Rick left for the food table with the girls while he and Nina stayed behind, making small talk, but he enjoyed it. For so long he'd feared that a woman might think he was coming on to her and not just being friendly. But Nina had a way about her that gave him no worries that she was looking for romance.

More at ease, he returned to their discussion. "I'm guessing our places are similar. Mine has three bedrooms and a good-sized dining room."

He doubted she cared, and he disliked small talk, too, but that's all he could come up with.

"Mine's similar. Would you like to see it?"

"Sure, but let me check on Kimmy first." He rose and spotted Angie returning with the girls. "Will you keep an eye on Kimmy for a few minutes? I'm going—"

"No problem." She flashed a playful wink. "Have fun."

Nina arched an eyebrow. "It's only… Never mind." She brushed her words away and rose. "We don't need to explain, do we?"

"Not at all." He enjoyed her lighthearted spirit and joined her on the sidewalk, heading to her home. Though he'd passed her house often, he'd never really noticed its homey look. It had a porch on half of the front and the other side, an overhung alcove with attractive wide windows. His home lacked the warmth and was more streamlined. Too much like him. "It has a friendly feel, Nina. Like you."

"Me?" Her voice rose. "I'm just boring."

"To yourself maybe, but not to me." Hearing his honesty startled him.

"Thank you, Doug." Her stunned expression set him back.

She opened the door, and they stepped inside. "This is the living room, naturally."

The size surprised him. "It's like a great room. I like the corner fireplace."

She didn't comment. "Dining room." She made a sweeping gesture.

He slipped his hands into his pockets, uneasy that he had no awareness of what she was thinking. He noted the wide archway added even more space to the already-large living area.

Nina gestured to the doorway leading from the dining room. "And the kitchen."

She stepped inside and he followed, noting numerous cabinets but minimal counter space and a pair of folding doors. "Is this a pantry?"

"I wish." She folded back the doors to expose a washer and dryer. "This is my laundry room." She gave a shrug. "No basement."

"Mine is a small room off the kitchen." He leaned his back against a counter and studied her a moment. "You have lots of room for one person. Are you anticipating finding someone to share it with?" He cringed. Why not just ask if she was engaged or dating someone?

"I'm not anticipating anything." Her tone had an edge. "I like the space."

He wanted to undo the damage. "You never know about the future."

A frown shot to her face. "No marriage plans in my future, if that's what you mean. None. Not interested."

He drew back, wishing he'd kept his mouth shut. "I'm sorry, Nina. That sounded crude and too nosy. I have no plans at the moment, either.

Once Kimmy's back with her mom, it's just me. That was an ignorant comment."

Her frown faded, replaced by an unreadable expression. "Doug, I've been married once. I don't think it's meant for me. Once is enough."

Though he reacted as if he understood, her sharp response sent a sliver of disappointment through his chest and left him even more curious.

"Back to the tour." She strode through the kitchen doorway to a short hallway on the opposite side of the house. "Three bedrooms. Right now the smallest is sort of an office with my computer and some exercise equipment. The middle size is a guest room." She raised her eyebrows. "Now all I need are guests. And the master bedroom is large and faces the back with a walk-in closet and master bath."

She didn't step inside but raced through her descriptions, gesturing as he glanced into the three rooms. Her manner had changed since he'd stupidly asked the personal question about her future plans. He'd messed up, but then he'd done that before. He mumbled something about the attractive rooms and watched her edge toward the front door.

Obviously she wanted out of the situation. He decided to give her a solution. "Thanks for the tour. I should get back to Kimmy."

She didn't say a word but headed for the door.

He followed her into the great room. "You have a nice place here, Nina."

She only nodded and opened the front door.

His chest constricted. He had no doubt this was the end of their amiable relationship. And he knew it was for the best. He had nothing to offer except his preoccupation with his sister's horrible situation and Kimmy's needs. Then he had his own feelings, ones he disliked more than he wanted to face. *Inadequacy* had never been a word in his life until now. But when he'd opened his mouth to repair the damage he couldn't even put a patch on it until he got himself and his head in the right place. Obviously a repair job was pointless. He'd made a mess of it, and of all things, he liked her.

Chapter Two

Despite her declaration to remain uninvolved, Doug's image dangled in Nina's thoughts like a mule's carrot. His smile, his lost look, his fleeting glances rolled into a tempting nugget in her imagination. She opened her computer to occupy her mind with something other than Doug but when she stared at the monitor, her mind segued back to the block party. For someone who could evaluate promotional programs and manage entire brands, she failed when it came to her own life.

Spending the morning with her thoughts spinning motivated her to break down the steps she used in her work to evaluate her own needs and goals. But the big question was how? How did she look with fresh eyes and see anything that wasn't tangled in her past?

She scooted her chair back and rose. Why did she waste time reliving her last conversation with Doug? She'd got in a huff, and when he left her house, she'd ushered him to the front door without a kind word, and the poor guy had no idea why. And she couldn't explain it, either. Yes, he'd brought up a bad time, but that had been years earlier. Nothing could be done, so why dwell on it?

She strode to the kitchen and poured coffee into a cup. The strong odor curled her nose so she poured it out, rinsed the cup and found a tea bag. Microwaves came in handy for a single cup of tea. Waiting, she opened the sliding door and gazed into the yard. Even though the season was late, she'd wanted to add some perennials that would come up next year. Angie's yard looked lovely with fall blossoms.

The buzzer sounded, and she headed back to her makeshift office with her cup of tea. Yet the tea didn't help, either. Her mind flew from one idea for a client to the block party. She'd met a few neighbors, saying hello or responding with "Yes, I'm new on the block," but still it was a beginning. She especially enjoyed meeting El. He embodied a rare spirit filled with wit, kindness and wisdom.

El had an innocence about him—a man who trusted his instinct and didn't question his decision to be friendly or look for motivation. That's where she had failed. Any question that delved too deeply into her personal hang-ups or sorrows invaded her comfort level and she assumed the person was nosy or prying. Doug's question had been general not probing.

Draining the last of her tea, she rose and set the empty cup in the kitchen, grabbed her house key and stepped outside. The quiet of the street spilled over her, as empty as her teacup. The block party had resounded with voices, children laughing and music playing on a speaker somewhere. A few people had danced in the circular area of the street.

How long had it been since she'd danced? Forever. She recalled Doug saying life had got in his way. She stood on her sidewalk, her eyes closed for a moment, picturing the friendly atmospherc of the Friday block party.

As she walked, she spotted El sitting on a wooden glider in his front yard. Though she regretted not having a treat to offer him, she headed that way. Flowers bloomed in his flower beds, and she wanted to ask about them. Maybe he could offer her ideas on what would be good to plant this time of year.

Thoughts returned again on her rudeness to Doug. She'd startled him as well as herself. Nearing El's, she realized her motivation for coming was feeling alone. El had mentioned loneliness once, and today it overwhelmed her, a strange emotion with no solution other than to seek company. For years, she'd avoided company after Todd left, saying she didn't care.

Her heart skipped as she neared Doug's house. His car sat back in the driveway signaling he was home, but she saw no sign of him. She should be relieved to avoid a confrontation, but instead, a guilty sting burned through her. She'd behaved terribly.

El saw her coming and raised his hand in greeting. She waved back, glad for the distraction. As she stepped onto his lawn, he rose, planting his feet on the ground while hoisting himself from the glider without losing his balance.

He grinned. "How are you this fine Sunday?"

She nodded at his welcome and ambled toward him, hoping to look casual and not unnerved. "Beautiful day, isn't it?"

"Couldn't ask the Lord for better."

The reference helped her understand El's ways. He lived by the rules that people of the church took for granted. She'd known a few things about faith once, but she'd let her curiosity die. Had her divorce triggered her hopelessness? She couldn't recall what ended her interest. Yet she sometimes envied those who had faith. They lived with the philosophy that life never ended. This world was only a stepping stone to something better. The idea that life held more than the here and now, though strange, had a comfortable ring to it. A spark warmed her again.

El patted the seat on the swing. "Join me a

minute." He grasped the arm and sank back onto the slats.

With her growing curiosity, she did as he suggested and sank beside him. "You have pretty flowers, El." She twisted on her hip to face him. "You don't mind that I call you El?"

"Mind." He tossed his head back with a chuckle. "That's my name, and I'm hanging on to it."

He made her grin. "Okay, then. In case you forgot, I'm Nina."

"Pretty name. I wouldn't forget that one." He gave her arm a pat. "Thank you for mentioning the flowers. My wife always urged me to plant flowers. I was smart enough to learn that urging was one of those things that women did rather than just demand their husbands do it."

This time she chuckled. "Did your wife have favorite flowers?"

"She sure did. She loved the ones that came up year after year. That's mainly what you're looking at—daisies, coneflowers, asters, and those purple ones are called catmint. I added a few geraniums. They're faithful flowers, growing in nearly every environment." He winked. "They're not fussy."

"That's one of the few flowers I know by name. But now I recognize the white daisies."

"Coneflowers are the colorful ones there." He pointed to a bed of daisy-like blossoms. "Pretty things in so many colors."

"I want to do some planting. I have a few clumps of flowers in the front. I'm not sure what they are, but…" She relaxed against the seat back. "I finally have my new house organized." She eyed him. "Sort of."

He chuckled, his gaze washing across her face as if he had questions but didn't ask.

"How did your meal go with Birdie on Friday?"

"Fine. I think she appreciated the company and that I accepted her invitation." He chuckled again. "She asked if we could eat together, but she didn't have a table or chairs. That means she sort of urged me to ask her." His eyes glinted with his joke before he leaned forward, his elbows on his knees, hands woven together. "Birdie's been standoffish until recently. That's a lonely life for a woman who still has years to enjoy each day."

His words swept over her. "To be honest, El, I've been somewhat that way, too."

He nodded while a faint crooked grin grew on his face. "I sensed that, Nina. You know, whatever happened in your past is just that. It's passed. Ahead of you is a future, but you have to participate in it." He stopped and shook his head. "This is just ramblings of an old man, but sometimes I see things and…" He sat a moment his head hanging. "I see you and sense you have regrets and sorrows that you're clinging to. Ask yourself if they're worth it."

Worth it? Though his first words rankled, she

forced herself to listen, and a sense of possibility hung over her, nebulous but there.

"Please forgive me. How you live your life is none of my business. Birdie got in trouble nosing around other people's lives, and I'm doing the same thing."

She touched his arm and squeezed. "El, you're not a gossip. You're not spreading rumors. You're talking to me like a father might. That's something I never had." The admission spilled ice water through her body. "You're right. I had a bad marriage, and I have other issues that formed my judgment. Marrying again is basically not a possibility. I guess the reality makes me a little empty…and what you just said. Lonely."

"Nothing could be so bad it stops you from falling in love again. Are you sure marriage is out of the question?"

His tender look rent her heart. "I'm sure. I'm sorry, but I don't want to talk about it. I know how I feel, and I think that's how it will be." Without warning, her gaze flashed back down the block toward Doug's. Her pulse skipped when she spotted him outside with Kimmy.

"Then I'll pray for you to find an answer to your problem, Nina. Do you pray?"

His question stopped her. She almost felt ashamed to answer him. "I've never learned to pray."

"You don't learn it, Nina. What are we doing right now?"

She eyed him, trying to decipher what he meant. Thoughts surged. They had talked about the flowers, her attitude toward marriage. "We've talked about a lot of things."

"Yes. That's it."

"That's it?" Her head spun. "Talking?"

"Yep. Prayer is just talking to God. Tell Him about your day. Ask Him for answers to your questions. Thank Him for His blessings. And then listen."

"Listen? That's the thing about prayer I don't understand. God doesn't speak. They say He's there. You know, sort of like the wind is there. We can't see it, but we feel it or we can see what it does."

"Yep, you got it. You can't see Him, but you can feel Him if you open your heart, but then that takes trust."

"It's hard to trust something or someone you don't know." She brushed a curl from her face.

"But it's not impossible. Think about things that you trust even though you don't know why or don't have the details. You trust your employer will pay you. Why? Because he said he would."

She shook her head. That was a given. Wasn't it? Maybe not. "You trust the sun will come up in the morning. Even if it's behind a cloud, you know it's there."

"But that's nature. It's always been that way."

"So has God, Nina. He was there before the sun was made."

A frown wrenched her face even though she tried to stop it.

"Do you have a Bible?"

Her back tensed. "No."

"I have Margie's. I think she'd like you to have it."

"Margie?"

"My wife's name. Marjorie. Most people called her Marge, but she was always Margie to me." A tender sweetness spread across his face.

The look touched her. "El, I couldn't take your wife's Bible."

"Why? She doesn't need it, Nina. She's sitting up there listening to the Lord, and He tells her all she needs to know. She's in her glory." He chuckled. "In her glory in Glory." He nodded as if he'd settled on an agreement with himself.

"But it's precious to you. A keepsake."

"It's more precious to me if someone's using it." He shifted on the seat, causing it to glide back and then forward. "Now I know you're not a Bible reader, but if you have questions or if you're curious, you can check the concordance and look up the exact topic you'd like to know about."

"You mean an index?"

He pushed himself forward again but this time

he rose. "You can call it that. It's right inside. Hang on a minute."

Before she could react, he headed toward the house on a mission. She'd never seen him move so fast. She lowered her head, sorting through all that had happened. Somehow she'd moved from flowers to faith without knowing how. Maybe that was one of those God things people talked about.

Guilt rattled up her spine. If she took his Bible, realizing she had little choice, what would make her read it? The possibility wavered over her.

"Here you go."

She jerked, unaware El had returned.

He extended the worn-looking Bible, and not knowing how to refuse, she grasped it. Hoping to make him happy, she opened it to the back and flipped through the topics with verses listed underneath—hardship, loyalty, prayer. She turned the pages back. Faith. She eyed the long row of verses. The first she spotted was Matthew 17:22. She eyed the preview. *He replied, "Because you have so little faith. I tell you the truth..."* The example stopped her cold. What? What was the truth?

"Is something wrong, Nina?"

She drew her head upward. "No. Not at all. I was thinking, I guess."

"Nothing wrong with that. I'm not rushing you. You have God's Word in your hands if you have any questions, and though I don't have all the answers, you're always welcome to ask me anything."

She rose, clutching the book, and gathered her wits. "Thank you, El. And I feel bad taking your—"

"It's an honor, Nina. Margie is smiling in heaven." His face brightened. "I know she's smiling."

How could she refuse his generous gift? "Thank you, El. May I kiss your cheek?"

"I'd love that, Nina."

She leaned forward and pressed her lips on his soft cheek. "Thank you for everything. I'll take your flower advice, and I promise... I'll keep the book handy. I'm sure one day—"

"I'm sure you will." His smile broadened. "I'm anxious to see those flowers, too."

The best part for now was the flowers. She was anxious to get to a nursery. Most plants were probably on sale, she hoped, and she'd save money as well as adorn her flower beds.

Hope. That had been a rare word in her vocabulary, but El's certainty that she would read the Bible made her grin. That was hope. And she had faith, too, but different. If she planted flowers in the fall, she had faith they would blossom in the spring or summer.

She tucked the Bible under her arm and headed down the sidewalk, aware that Doug and Kimmy were on the other side. Although her mind was as ragged as it had been when she stepped outside, a sense of peace had sneaked into her being. Though it would be short-lived, something about El gave her a sense of security and hope. Hope? She'd had so little, but today she had a touch of it.

As she drew closer to Doug, her peace sank into confusion. She could hardly ignore him, but what could she say? She marched along, wishing he wouldn't notice her.

Doug sat on a porch step keeping an eye on Kimmy working on her first school project collecting bugs. Offering science classes seemed a little early for second graders. But what did he know? He shook his head, hoping Kimmy didn't get stung or bit by something, but her search was in the name of homework so he didn't say a word.

Trying to be a good father-type for Kimmy, he usually joined her in projects, but today his thoughts weighted him down. He'd done something to upset Nina. His questions had been too personal for her, he guessed. Something...

When he looked up, his heart stopped. Nina appeared across the street like a vision, but he knew she was real. Her long hair hung to her shoulders in waves. It fluttered in the breeze, and he longed to brush it from her cheek. He faltered, unsure of what he wanted to do.

When she glanced his way, he raised his hand,

a natural instinct that he hadn't monitored. Anticipating she'd ignore his greeting, his chest constricted when she crossed the street. Though curious where she'd been, he wouldn't ask. That question could be too personal, also.

"I noticed you outside with Kimmy. How are you?"

He wanted to tell her he was confused, but he changed his answer to something safe. "Good. The weather motivated me to come outside."

She strode up to Kimmy. "What are you looking for?"

"Bugs." She grinned.

"Bugs. Hmm? Any special reason or are you just curious?"

"School started and I'm in the second grade."

"Second grade. And you have to find bugs." Nina tilted her head.

"Homework." Kimmy's face glowed. "It's for our science class."

"Did you find any ladybugs?" Nina looked at the insects in Kimmy's jar.

"Those ones who fly away home 'cuz their house is on fire?"

The girl's face lit with a smile, and Nina grinned. "I'm sure those are the ones."

Kimmy shook her head. "I only found two ants, a fly and something with lots of legs." She held up her jar with air holes punched in the lid.

"I have ladybugs at my house. They like flowers, and even though I have only a few blossoms, I see insects there."

Doug watched, amazed at Nina's lighthearted banter with no hint of anger. Still, she was talking with Kimmy, not him. But she'd stopped by and that was something.

"Uncle Doug, can I go to Nina's and get some ladybugs?" She gave him a beseeching look.

He couldn't hold back his grin. "I don't want to hinder research. I suppose you can if Nina doesn't mind."

Nina tousled Kimmy's hair. "Come down whenever you'd like. I'm home for the evening."

He opened his mouth but sat speechless.

"Doug." Nina closed the distance and sat beside him, running her fingers through her hair. "I owe you an apology. I'm sorry for the way I acted on Friday."

"You don't owe me—"

"I owe you respect and friendship. You've been kind, and I enjoyed your company until my fortress rose to shield me. It does that sometimes without my realizing it. You didn't deserve to be treated that way."

Although her fortress aroused his curiosity, relief flooded him, and he released a strangled breath. "Thank you. I don't need to forgive you, but I will. We all let our protective devices appear sometimes. I've done it myself. You know I question my ability with…" He feared Kimmy would hear her name so he tilted his head. "I would love to have confidence in my parenting skills. Women seem to have those built in."

Nina's crooked grin preceded her head shake. "We are frightened, too, Doug. Women know they're supposed to have inborn motherly instincts, but that's a myth. We cover up our worries and plow ahead. We read books and ask friends who won't think we're silly. In a way, it's like anything new. We do the best we can. Whatever you've done, Doug, has been right from all I see. Kimmy seems happy and healthy. You can't ask for more."

As if she'd heard her name, Kimmy came skipping toward them. "Can we go now?"

"We have company, my girl."

"But we can take her along." She beckoned to them.

Nina grinned. "Thank you for inviting me to join you."

Missing the point, Kimmy gave her a big smile. "You're welcome."

He gulped down his chuckle and patted Nina's hand. "Sorry. I think it takes a few years for a sense of humor to develop."

"It's funnier that way." Nina rose and extended her hand. "Friends."

"Positively."

"Good. Now I'd better go home since I'm

expecting company." She stepped toward Kimmy, but he stopped her.

"What's in your hand?"

She glanced down as if she'd forgotten.

"It looks like a—"

"Bible." She took a step closer. "It was El's wife's. He wanted me to have it since I don't own one."

His back straightened. "Did you mind?"

She shook her head. "I would expect nothing less from him. He lives his faith. I've never learned what that is, and I suppose he thought he would help me understand."

He didn't know what to say so he just gave a nod.

"I'll see you later, right?"

"For sure. Kimmy has her heart set on it." So did he.

Nina gave a wave and returned to Kimmy's side. She gave her a pat and whispered something in her ear before heading home.

He watched her go, both relieved and confused. He couldn't be happier to see her with the Bible, and he prayed she would look inside and grow in faith. He should do the same with all his doubts and worries. And maybe his new concern was one of those useless worries. Though something about Nina was lovely and intriguing, something else still blocked her from living fully. That's what he sensed, and it saddened him.

Chapter Three

Kimmy skipped along the sidewalk and paused when she reached Nina's. Doug caught up and faced the house, hoping his big mouth didn't result in another problem as it had at the block party. Though she'd apologized, he realized his question about the possibility of someone living with her had been blunt. Rude, really. It had been none of his business. On top of that, his ulterior motive was also inappropriate. Why not just ask if she were seeing someone? Or was that also blunt? Women confused him.

"Come on, Uncle Doug." Kimmy skipped halfway up the front walk and beckoned to him.

Before he took a step, Kimmy had already turned her attention to a few clumps of flowers in the beds along the house. He gazed at her creeping around the leaves, loving her curiosity and eagerness to do homework, hoping her attitude would last a lifetime. Having a good work ethic helped a career. He shook his head, realizing how far in the future he'd gone. Instead he should focus on his own future.

"Coming in?"

He faced Nina standing in the doorway. "Stay right here, Kimmy, and then let me know when you've finished.

Nina swung the door wider, and again he wished he had a larger living room. When he stepped in, she motioned toward the sofa, her only seating besides the recliner.

Still in the doorway, Nina leaned out. "The door's open, Kimmy. Come in when you're done."

His senses heightened. "Something smells delicious."

"Good." She turned from the door. "I'm making enough for all of us, but it'll be a while. It's in a slow cooker. Are you starving?"

Even if he was, he wouldn't admit it. He shook his head.

"Good." She sank into her recliner. "I thought if I have leftovers, I'd take them to El later tonight so he will have a surprise home-cooked dinner."

Doug couldn't imagine having home-cooked meals delivered to his door. His own simple recipes didn't thrill him. "You're a good person, Nina."

She lifted an eyebrow. "Thanks. I wish—"

What did she wish? His mouth opened, then closed. He had to learn not to ask questions or make comments. She'd made it clear her life and problems were not up for discussion. "We ate lunch before we came so we're good." His eyes shifted from her to the Bible beside her.

Nina studied him, as if noticing his distraction. "You asked about the Bible earlier." She rested her hand on the black leather book sitting on the table. "I'm not a religious person. Never brought up that way." She shrugged. "El must have thought I needed to take a look. I couldn't say no, but it's all rather difficult for me."

She looked away a moment, and though he sensed he should respond, he was at a loss for words.

"I will admit that El had some solid attitudes about God and faith. Things I'll ponder, I think."

"Faith is different for each person. I think it happens in its own way. I grew up in a home where church was a normal Sunday activity. I went to Sunday school and sometimes the adult services. I believe, but even I find it easy to skip church sometimes, especially since I moved. I need to look for a home church." A rivulet of guilt ran through him. "I've passed so many here in Owosso. I think there's one on every other corner." Though he chuckled, his discomfort didn't fade. "I try to go most Sundays when I have a church family."

"Family?" She shrugged.

"It feels like a family and it's a meaningful break in the week."

"I imagine it is. Music and readings. Those things can draw a mind away from day-to-day troubles." She patted the Bible and pulled her hand away as if it had burned her. "Any news from Kimmy's mom?"

He drew his focus from the Bible to Nina, noting a look of discomfort on her face. "I talked with her yesterday." A pang of sadness whipped through him, mixed with concern. "She's in therapy now, but I don't think she can stay by herself yet even if she comes home. It sounded as if she'll go into an inpatient rehabilitation facility for physical and occupational therapy before they release her." His throat caught as he absorbed the issues continuing to grow. "Our mother lives a number of miles away but she wouldn't be much help, and I work every day."

"I'm sure a facility would be the best for her, Doug. She'll get good treatment." She searched his face, her own growing taut before she glanced out the window. "Doug, you've never mentioned Kimmy's father. Is he anywhere in the picture?"

His mood darkened. "Never. He's never seen Kimmy. I don't know if he ever knew about her. Roseanne never talks about him."

"She'd never married or—?"

"That's right. She took a chance, and Kimmy

happened. She won't talk about it so I don't know a thing about him."

"That's hard." She appeared thoughtful. "Does Kimmy ever ask about him?"

He shrugged, hoping to hide his dark feelings. "I guess she has but Roseanne concocted some story. I think she said he died."

"One day when she's older Kimmy will want details. How he died. When? Did he love her? All those things we all want to know about our parents."

"I agree, but Roseanne only shakes her head and ignores me. She'll do what's right when Kimmy's older, I hope."

"I think she will. Truth from a mother with her child is important."

Letting the subject fade seemed his best move, and he gazed out the window and a grin broke the tension. "Kimmy's chasing something in one of the bushes."

Nina craned her neck to look outside "She seems to be doing well. She's adjusted. It's better for her to stay with you." Nina looked away a moment. "And you know, Doug, Kimmy's a bright little girl, and I fear she might feel too much responsibility and even guilt if she went home with her mother still needing care. I don't suppose you want to hear that."

"I've thought about that, too." He forced his eyes to stay connected with hers. "But I'm worried how to work it out. I can't take a leave, Nina. It's not feasible. Yet I'm the only one Rose-anne can count on."

"I wish I had the answers." A distant look filled her eyes, but then she brightened. "I realize we've only met, but she's a sweet girl and... I'd be willing to help in any way I can."

Her concern for Kimmy touched him, and he wondered why she didn't have children, but he knew better than to even hint at the question. "I'm sure you're right, and thanks for your offer."

The subject weighed on him, and he opened his mind to allow another thought to slip from his memory. "Isn't Angie and Rick's wedding soon? I overheard something on Friday. For a while, I thought they were already married, but obviously they're not. He always goes home at night."

Nina laughed. "They're ones who follow their religion, I think." She shook her head. "But that's wise."

She quieted again, and he wished they could recapture the easy, casual relationship they'd had when they first met.

Finally she broke the silence. "I was surprised when I received a wedding invitation. We've only known each other a short time, but we clicked, I guess. I like Angie and Rick. Carly's a doll, too. She'll be their flower girl."

"I thought flower girls were toddlers who cry and run back to their moms."

She laughed. "Sometimes, yes, but this is a wonderful way to include her in the ceremony."

"It is. I was being silly." He grinned, glad his remark had broken the tension.

She studied him for a moment. "Do you get upset by personal questions?"

He managed to lasso his laugh, recalling her idiosyncrasy. "Not usually, but I'd say it depends on what kind of personal question."

She sent him a half grin and glanced out the window again. "I know you're single, but I can't help but wonder why."

"I ask myself the same question. I mentioned once that life got in the way. And there's truth to that. My dad was ill for a long time, and I did what I could to help my parents. Mom wasn't that healthy either, and Dad needed to be lifted or helped to stand. He lost both legs to diabetes." Those horrible days resurfaced, bringing pain with them. "Dad was a man's man. Wouldn't listen to my mom or the doctor's warnings. He thought he could beat all illnesses, but he couldn't. Strange how we do that, isn't it? We know what's best, but we ignore it."

Her face darkened a moment, and he feared he'd done it again. "Nina, I'm sorry if I—"

She held up her hand. "No. It wasn't what you said. There's truth to that. I've been bitter for years over my failed marriage, and yet when you said we know what's best but we ignore it, it struck home. The divorce was probably for the best under the circumstances."

Questions flew to his tongue but again he refrained from uttering even a small question. Her marriage seemed to cause the last bugaboo, and he'd already spilled out too much of his life. He forgot they were virtual strangers. They'd met a short time ago, and yet it seemed as if it had been forever.

She eyed him as if wondering why he'd become silent.

He buried his question. "It's good sometimes to look back with fresh eyes. I think with most things, time clears our heads and we can face things differently. We let the blame go and focus on the result or the possibilities."

"Possibilities. That's sort of like hope, isn't it?"

"I suppose it is." He dragged his fingers through his hair. "I still hold out hope that one day in the near future I'll find the right person." What had he said? His mouth flapped without control. He'd spent much of his life preoccupied with everyone but himself. Where had those feelings come from?

And yet he knew. He studied her, admiring her light brown eyes that crinkled when she smiled and her intriguing wavy hair.

"For some people that's a real hope." She lifted a finger. "Let me check on the time. I still need to add something to the slow cooker." She rose and hurried away.

He watched her disappear beyond the door, as if she anticipated another question from him and was dodging it. He wished he could control his mouth and his heart. Nina looked uneasy, and he wished he knew what he could do to make their friendship as relaxed as it had been before.

He rose, perplexed, and wandered to the window, amazed that Kimmy spent so much time and patience in search of bugs. He shook his head. His patience ran amok more times than not. He should learn something from his young niece.

"I'm back."

He turned and was struck by how lovely Nina was. She walked with an air of confidence, yet she had an amiable aura. Despite her discomfort with personal subjects, she reached out to Kimmy in a sweet manner. That's what attracted him.

Nina joined him by the window. "I suppose we could go out and look for bugs, too."

"Or just watch. I don't want to ruin Kimmy's fun."

She chuckled. "Are you one of those men afraid of spiders?"

"I'm not talking."

With no other comment, she stepped outside to the porch, where two canvas chairs sat on the far end. He settled into one and Nina followed.

"What do you do if Kimmy's sick or if you have to work overtime?"

He drew in a breath, hating to think of those situations. "Thank the Lord, they've been rare, but I had to take off work or see if I could get a neighbor to step in for me. In my previous home, I had an older woman close by who usually volunteered. She was a blessing."

"You know I can often work at home, Doug. If you ever need someone in a pinch—"

"I couldn't ask you to do that, but thanks for offering. I just pray that she stays healthy, and I can get off work on time. They have a latchkey program at her school so Roseanne had her in that program until she could pick her up. It was only for an hour or so."

"If you're sure, but just in case…" She rose and headed into the house.

His jaw sagged at her quick departure. In a moment, she reappeared and handed him a small card. He glanced at it, surprised she had a business card. "I see you're a public relations consultant. That sounds interesting."

"That's why I can work from home at times. It's a lot of computer work. As long as I get it done and it's good, that's all that counts."

"Can you find me a job like that?" Feeling relief, he sensed their relationship had smoothed out again. He tucked the card into his pocket, pleased to see her cell phone number on it.

"Look, Uncle Doug."

"I see you found a ladybug."

"Two of them. Look."

He slipped his arm around Kimmy and gave her a hug. "Your teacher will be very happy with all the insects you captured."

Nina glanced at her watch. "I think it's time to get cleaned up for dinner. The food should be ready soon."

Doug loved Nina's manner with Kimmy. He let the two go ahead of him before joining them inside, enveloped in a cozy feeling too often alien to him. The idea of being a family and having children wrapped around his mind and left him with a sense of wholeness. The sensation gave him pause. He'd become too enamored of Nina, and he needed to sort out his feelings. Was it her kindness to Kimmy that brought up these emotions? Or was he truly altering his attitude about relationships...and marriage?

Nina hit Save on her computer and rose. Her eyes burned from staring at the monitor. She'd worked at home all day, and in the quiet, she'd accomplished one large task for her new client, but she had more to do.

She sank into her easy chair. Though things

had gone smoothly on Sunday with Doug, he hadn't contacted her since. Four days had passed with nothing. She'd thought their friendship had solidified with her apology and Doug's positive reaction.

When she lifted the footrest lever, she dropped back and closed her eyes, needing to sort her feelings. The word *friendship* struck her, but something deeper inched into her emotions. Getting involved again frightened her, and she'd set her mind to stay away from even a hint of commitment. Yet, Doug had come along and the idea of companionship cheered her. It aroused a sense of hope that Doug often talked about.

Since she'd moved to Lilac Circle, she had made friends with Angie and El and maybe that was enough. But as soon as she let the thought breathe, she knew the answer. She'd regret it if she and Doug didn't become true friends.

Friends, even good friends, could enjoy each other's company without calling it a date. Going to dinner together, talking on the porch, those were pleasant events without imposing two lives into one. That's what marriage was. The willingness to give of yourself and be one. She could stand on her own without anything more than an enjoyable friendship. The idea sent tension out the window. Good friends. Best friends, maybe. Platonic. That was the word. Platonic friendship. She blew a stream of air from her lungs.

Now to believe it and act on it.

As the friendship idea drifted, Angie's wedding came to mind. Though Angie had addressed it to her and a guest, she had mailed her RSVP indicating she would attend alone. Her shoulders heaved. Being alone at a wedding made her cringe. She would feel like an elderly maiden aunt who was parked in a chair and everyone had fun around her. What could she do to get out of it now? Illness? She could fake that, but it seemed so obvious. Her shoulder twitched again, and she veered her gaze out the window.

When she shifted her eyes, they lit on the bible. Margie's bible. El shouldn't have given it to her. Giving it to someone who would use it made more sense.

Yet her eyes remained on the book, and the verse she'd spotted at El's came to mind. She flipped to the back and turned pages until she spotted the reference, and then searched through the scripture until she found the verses—Matthew 17:20.

He said: "Because you have so little faith, I tell you the truth. If you have faith as small as a mustard seed, you can say to this mountain, "Move from here to there" and it will move. Nothing will be impossible for you.

But who was the He referred to in the verse? She moved her eyes upward and found her answer. Jesus. Jesus said with the tiniest bit of faith nothing was impossible. How could that be? She closed her eyes. A mustard seed was minute, but she couldn't claim to have even that amount of faith.

Her cell phone's ringtone sounded from a distance, and she slipped the Bible onto the table, dropped the footrest and hurried to the computer table in her office. She viewed a number she didn't recognize. It persisted. She hit talk and said hello.

"Nina, this is Doug."

Her heart lurched. "Is something wrong?" Her head spun—how did he have her number? Right, the business card.

"Nothing horrible. I've been asked—that's a nice way to put it—to work overtime tomorrow. I have a meeting in the morning and a huge project to get ready. I hate to ask, but—"

"Doug." Her heart slowed to a trot, knowing Kimmy was fine. "I volunteered. I don't mind. I'm going to the office in the morning and I'll be working at home the rest of the day. Kimmy will be fine with me."

"Are you sure?" The question rang with concern.

"I won't indulge you with a response." She

cleared her throat with as much drama as she could, hoping he recognized she was teasing him.

"Okay, I get you." Relief sounded in his tone. "I'll stop by tonight with the info you'll need, and I'll go into the school when I pick her up today and leave your name so they'll know I sent you."

"Good, because I don't want to be arrested for kidnapping."

He chuckled. "Thanks so much. By the way, I'm sorry I haven't seen you since Sunday. Once again life happened. I had to spend time with my mother on the phone, and then Kimmy and I went there one evening. She's having some health issues, and I'm trying to convince her to sell the house and move into an assisted living facility."

"Any progress?"

"Mom isn't the easiest to convince. It's frustrating."

She recognized the weariness in his voice. "I can imagine, and with her living a distance away, it's even more complex."

"Thanks for understanding." His contrite tone had brightened. "I'll drop by tonight."

The conversation ended, and she headed back to the chair, grateful that her work allowed her to spend time at home. And now with Kimmy, it answered Doug's need. A sense of purpose eased through her as she tilted back in her chair. She closed her eyes while visions of her new life spread around her. She'd see Doug tonight and spend time with Kimmy. What could be better? A platonic relationship seemed perfect.

Hearing the doorbell, Nina dropped the footrest again and bounded from the chair, startled that she'd fallen asleep. Confused, she eyed her watch as she opened the door.

"Hope I didn't interrupt." Angie grinned and took a step forward, anticipating being invited in.

"You didn't." She shifted back and beckoned Angie inside. "In fact, I'm glad you came." Nina swung her arm toward the recliner. "I'd fallen asleep in my chair."

"I'm so sorry I woke you." Angie frowned. "So what's stressing you out?"

Angie's questioning look caused Nina to shake her head. "Nothing. Why would you ask that? My eyes were tired. I've been staring at a monitor all day."

Angie chuckled. "It's a good excuse."

Nina ignored the comment and motioned to a chair. "Please have a seat."

She looked behind her and settled on the edge of the sofa. "I can't stay long, but I finally got around to checking the RSVPs and I noticed you only put down one person attending." She tilted her head, her eyes questioning.

"That's correct. There's no law, right?" Nina flashed a grin, though uncomfortable with Angie's reaction. "I'm not dating anyone, and I decided it was easier just to come alone."

"You can, but it's more fun when you have a friend with you. Do you like to dance?"

Angie's question stung. "I used to. It's been a long time."

"It's like riding a bike. You never forget how to do that."

Her attempt at humor failed. "I'll keep that in mind if the opportunity arises."

Angie rose. "I must have sounded pushy, Nina. Forgive me. I would love to see you have fun. I really like you."

"Thanks." She stood and rested her hand on Angie's shoulder. "But I think I'll come alone."

"Okay, but...what about Doug? He's a great guy and a neighbor. If we'd known him better, we might have invited him, too. In fact, there's your answer."

Whether she came alone or with someone wouldn't ruin the wedding reception. "Angie. I've already decided that I'm not asking anyone."

Angie studied her a moment as if ready to rebut. "Okay, if you're that determined, but I'll put you down for two just in case." She gave a one-shoulder shrug and turned toward the door before she wiggled her fingers in a wave. "See you later."

Exasperation bristled along Nina's arms as she said goodbye and watched her go. Maybe Angie was teasing, but why couldn't she make her own decisions without people pressuring her?

After stepping back through the doorway, she sank into her comfy chair. Bring a date? Angie assumed Doug was the only guy she knew well enough to ask. That was true, but she had never asked anyone for a date, and she wasn't starting now.

She shook her head. As for Doug, she already had concerns about her feelings. Asking him would be truly stupid.

As she tossed herself back, she hit the foot-rest lever. Maybe she could fall asleep again and awake convinced that Angie's visit was a bad dream.

Who was she kidding?

She closed her eyes, and her senses returned. What was she fighting? Angie hadn't suggested a date. She'd suggested an escort. Friends sometimes did that for friends.

Friends. The word rolled around in her mind. Minutes ago she'd thought the solution had been found. Platonic friends. Then what was the probem? She closed her eyes, releasing a sigh that rattled through her chest. She could fool others but not herself. Having Doug escort her, in reality, tempted her emotions. One day, he would face his own reality and want a family. If she fell in love with Doug, he could walk away as Todd had done when he learned she couldn't bear a child. Her chest constricted. And he should walk away if he wanted a family. She couldn't chance it.

* * *

After working without a break, Nina checked her watch. One. She needed to pick up Kimmy at school between three and three-thirty. Fatigued again, and not only from the monitor. She felt plain old tired. Her sleep the night before had been restless. She thanked Angie for that. Why had she made a big deal about attending the wedding alone? Yes, she would mess up the table seating. Most everyone attended as couples, so the tables usually seated eight or ten. She'd make it seven or nine. She managed a chuckle. Maybe someone's maiden aunt needed a seat.

She made her way to the kitchen, longing for something to distract her. The refrigerator didn't pose any invitation as she gazed inside. The few cookies still in the jar she'd kept for Kimmy. Crackers? With what? Peanut butter, but she ran out a few days before. Maybe a trip to the grocery store would do it.

Instead she opened the back door and stepped outside, her eyes grazing the landscape. She'd done nothing about the perennials, and soon it would be too late. She hurried back in, grabbed her cell phone and purse and slipped into her car, recalling a garden shop not too far away. Soon she was pulling into the parking lot. After studying two rows of flowers, she spotted the coneflowers and hoisted a plant into her basket while her mind slipped to Kimmy. Time was ticking away, and she didn't want to scare her or disappoint Doug by being late. With time on her mind, she spotted a sales clerk and caught her attention. "I'm in a new house without much landscaping, and I'm checking perennials but I want to make sure it's not too late to plant. Can you tell me?"

"Sure. You have coneflowers there. It's a good choice. They're hardy flowers, and in Zone 5 the fall months are perfect for planting."

She thanked the salesclerk and then asked directions to find the daisies.

The woman beckoned her to follow. With her guidance, she set three pots of daisies into the basket. Finally she circled back and grabbed three more colorful coneflowers to brighten her garden and her life.

She paid the bill, her mind everywhere but on her purchases. After she arrived home and unloaded, she realized Kimmy would already be waiting for her. Angry at her carelessness, she dashed to her car and headed down Oliver Street.

When she spotted the redbrick building, darkened with age, she slowed and pulled into the pickup lane. Only a few children were outside waiting, a couple others were getting into cars, but Kimmy wasn't among them. Panicking, she pictured Doug's frantic face and felt nailed to the seat. She sat a moment deciding what to do. Her only choice was to go inside. She drove to the parking lot and slipped out as her nerves set in.

What would she do if Kimmy had been picked up by someone else. Kidnapped? Her carelessness rent her heart.

Breathless, she darted along the inside corridor, following the sign to the office. As soon as she reached the door, she spotted Kimmy. Her legs weakened as relief spread over her.

Kimmy's eyes widened as she ran to her. "I thought you forgot me."

"I'd never do that, Kimmy." The words reverberated through her chest. She gave her a hug, noticing tears on Kimmy's cheeks. Nina's heart wrenched. "I'm sorry, sweetie. I would never forget you." Her throat closed as she struggled to continue. "I went to the nursery for flowers and time ran away from me." She tilted her head. "But I'm here now." *Thank You* soared above her and stopped her cold. *Thank You.* Had she prayed? Warmth spread through her body as her fears flew away.

She pulled herself from the sensation, noticing a questioning look from the woman behind the counter. "I'm sorry I'm late. Doug Billings gave you my name, I think. I'm here for Kimmy. He had to work overtime today."

The woman gave her a frown and checked a list near the phone and nodded. "You are?"

"Nina Jerome. Doug and I are neighbors."

The woman nodded. "We have to be careful, and we also ask that you be on time."

"Yes, I know. It won't happen again. I guarantee." She meant every word.

The woman gave a faint nod. "Kimmy, you can leave now and have a good weekend, okay?"

Kimmy grinned. "Okay."

"And do you have all of your belongings?"

She nodded to the woman while Nina stepped away, wanting to escape before the woman had her scrubbing boards or banging erasers.

Kimmy caught up with her in the hallway "This weekend I have to find different kinds of leaves and things that grow on trees and bushes." She adjusted her backpack. "Can we find them in your yard?"

"We sure can." Nina slipped her arm around Kimmy's shoulders and guided her outside.

When Kimmy spotted the car, she bolted ahead, and Nina had a hard time keeping up. Like a father, Doug had put the booster seat into the back of her car, and Kimmy slipped in and locked the seat belt. Captured by the image of Doug with his arms embracing a child of his own, Nina's heart grew heavy. If only... Not wanting the thought to ruin her day, she headed for the driver's seat and turned the key.

On the way home, she thought about the cookies she'd saved for Kimmy, but other than those, she had no after-school snacks for her. Her mind drifted until Kimmy broke her train of thought.

"Can we plant your flowers when we get back?

Carly got to help Angie plant the flowers. She told me."

Competition. Nina grinned. Though she liked the idea, today it wasn't practical. "It's late today, but let's plan it for another day—maybe tomorrow—and you can tell Carly you helped me plant flowers. Instead, let's do your homework. That will be fun, but first we'll stop at the store for a treat."

Kimmy's face brightened. "I like treats."

So did she, except for the calories. Again an image of Doug entered her mind, his smile the best treat she'd had in years.

She shook her head and pulled into a grocery store. Kimmy unhooked her seat belt, slipped outside, and they headed into the store. She guided Kimmy to healthy snacks and was pleased when she thought of string cheese. Kimmy liked those and peanut butter crackers. She selected multigrain. Another good choice.

In minutes, they were back in the car and pulling into her driveway. Kimmy lugged the grocery bag from the backseat, and they hurried inside for the snack and then the homework project.

Once in the yard, Kimmy slowed, her expression thoughtful. "Do you like my uncle Doug?"

Like? The question startled her, and her chest tightened. "I think he's a very nice man, and I like you, too." Her heart thudding, she studied Kimmy's expression. "Why do you ask?"

"He's happier since he met you. I'm glad you like him 'cuz I think he likes you…a lot."

Heat rushed up her neck and warmed her cheeks. "Thank you, Kimmy. It's always nice to be liked. I'm sure lots of people like you."

Kimmy looked thoughtful. "But I think you make Uncle Doug happier."

She made Doug happier? He made her happier, too, but this topic had to stop before she lost it. "Look there, Kimmy." She pointed to the grass, grateful she'd spotted the pinecone. "Do you know what that is?"

"An acorn?" Kimmy eyed the cone a moment before shaking her head. "It's the other one. A…"

"Right. It's a pinecone. People make Christmas decorations out of them."

Her eyes widened. "They do?" She picked up the cone and studied it. "How?"

Her brain went into gear. "I think they spray them with gold paint and tie a red bow on top. They can add artificial holly berries or other little Christmas symbols."

"Can we make some for Christmas?"

"Christmas?" Nina's heart weighted, doubting Kimmy would still be with Doug then. The old familiar loneliness spread through her. She drew in a breath. "We'll have to wait and see. You might be home and busy with your mom."

A shadow slipped across Kimmy's face. "But I

could come and visit Uncle Doug." Hope washed away the gloom. "Then we could make them."

"We probably could." Nina stepped away, needing to avoid the emotions barraging her. She'd never given the future much thought, and she didn't want to start now.

Her mind bogged with Kimmy's questions and especially her earlier comment. If a child noticed Doug seemed happier when she was around him, wouldn't everyone spot it? She hadn't known him long enough to notice a change in his behavior. Her heart pressed against her chest as if it were paper and could tear through. One thing she couldn't do was offer Doug empty hope. She bit the edge of her lip unable to face her own emptiness.

Kimmy dashed around the yard collecting leaves from shrubs and plants, even two blades of crabgrass that Nina needed to attend to. She watched the girl, caught up in her excitement and energy. Though she was only thirty-four, her energy had dropped a couple of notches each year. She'd be bedridden by fifty if she didn't perk up and find enjoyment in life.

A sound drew her attention, and she felt her pocket. She dug into it and pulled out her cell phone. This time she recognized the phone number. "Hi, Doug."

"How's it going? Did you pick up Kimmy?"

"Sure did." Her pulse kicked into a high gear.

"We had healthy snacks, and now we're doing her homework."

Doug chuckled. "What is it this time?"

"Here, you can ask Kimmy." She beckoned to her, and she bounced forward, a smile brimming on her face.

"Hello."

Whatever Doug asked or said, Kimmy rattled on about the snacks and homework, along with a list of what she'd found.

Nina's cheeks warmed again, seeing joy in the child's face. She amazed her, rolling with catastrophes better than most adults. While her mother was miles away, badly injured, Kimmy had dealt with the situation like a professional, making the best of her time with Doug without complaint. Even without fear.

She longed to cope with upheaval as well as Kimmy. If she'd done so, today she would be ready to make changes in her life, to move on and find happiness once again. Instead, she'd clung to her pitiful past and feelings of abandonment in the way someone would cherish old pictures.

Kimmy returned the phone to her, and she lifted it to her ear. "We're doing fine, Doug."

"Good. I hope to get out of here by seven-thirty. Eight at the latest."

She pictured his face, his eyes crinkling at the edges as he talked, the lock of hair that sometimes dipped to his forehead, the five o'clock shadow she found so appealing. "We're fine, Doug. Really."

"I owe you one, Nina. Ask and it's yours. Anything."

His offer sent prickles up her arms. "You might be sorry you said that."

"Never. I'll see you later."

They disconnected, and she approached Kimmy with Doug's offer ringing in her ears.

Angie's insistence that she have an escort for the wedding had bugged her, and naturally Angie thought of Doug. But Doug had already been embedded in her mind since they'd spent so much time together. Everything had been innocent and mainly involving Kimmy. The wedding didn't involve Kimmy. In fact he'd have to hire a babysitter. She couldn't ask him.

I owe you one, Nina. Ask and it's yours. Anything. Anything. But escorting her to a wedding certainly wasn't what he had in mind. But...what had he meant? He said *anything*.

Her mind spun, and she closed her eyes. Truth was, the more she thought of it, she disliked attending the reception alone. A wedding service, maybe, but the celebration? A party? Alone would be a downer. Still asking Doug...that would take gumption on her part and even a bit of faith.

The idea settled in her mind. She'd already

talked to God once today. Maybe, just maybe, another little chat might give her unexpected courage.

The whole idea spread through her like puzzle pieces. She'd always been good with them except the puzzles of her life. That was one she hadn't conquered yet. But maybe, just maybe…

Chapter Four

Doug leaned back in his office chair and eyed the stack of paperwork that he'd nearly conquered. He rubbed the back of his neck, kneading out the knots, and checked his watch with blurred vision. He'd stared at the computer too long, and though he still had portions of the documents, he couldn't face another moment. He had to consider Kimmy's needs.

Nina slipped into his mind again, and his pulse snagged. He'd never met a woman so unselfish with her time. Not only had she spent hours with Kimmy already, she had volunteered to spend more. What kind of woman did that?

A grin pranced to his lips. A woman who loved children. He nodded. That was it. He'd watched her with Kimmy, and she was a natural and very creative with her. He loved that. Again, his pulse stumbled as he faced the truth. He liked Nina.

Liked her a lot. More than any other woman he'd known. But then she was easy to lov…like.

And now Angie had offered him an opening. Her wedding. He'd never expected to receive an invitation with the stipulation he escort Nina. All he needed now was the nerve to ask her. The wedding would be a way to know her better and to see her in a social setting. The neighborhood outdoor party had been the only social situation where they'd been together, and she seemed somewhat withdrawn. He had so much to learn about her. Only then could he really let his thoughts take flight. He drew in a breath as he admitted his failure. They'd already taken flight without his permission. So unlike him.

He shook his head to clear his thoughts and flicked through the documents, confident he could finish in the morning before his meeting. He riffled the pages and tapped them into a neat stack before slipping them into a folder and dropping them into his work tray. As he logged off the computer, his stomach rumbled, reminding him he'd rushed through a flavorless sandwich at noon, and now eating a good meal sounded great.

Tonight cooking was out of the question, but take-home was perfect, and Kimmy loved Chinese food. Tasty food with no work hugged his thoughts. He grasped his cell phone and located Nina's number. His heart lurched when she answered on the second ring.

"Nina, this is Doug."

She chuckled. "I saw your face on my phone."

His chest tightened. "My face?" He'd seen hers so often in his mind, but on his—

"I snapped a photo of you one day in the yard when you weren't looking. Now I can see your picture when you call."

A grin stole to his lips again. "Lucky you." He hoped he sounded lighthearted. Although in his ears, he sounded breathless. Exactly how he felt.

She chuckled. "How's work?"

"Done for the night. Did Kimmy eat dinner? I—"

"Doug, I'm sorry. We had a late snack and I haven't done a thing yet, but I can feed her for you if—"

"Don't be sorry. That's good. I thought I'd pick up Chinese." He hesitated before barreling ahead. "Do you like it?"

"Love it."

"Great. I always bring home too much for us, and I'd love to share. You won't have to worry about cooking tonight...unless you need a break from Kimmy."

"From Kimmy? Never."

"How about me?"

She laughed. "A break? Not at all. I look forward to seeing you...and the Chinese food, especially egg rolls."

"Our favorite, too." Though she'd stumbled

over her words, he was glad he'd asked. His shoulders straightened. "You'll see me and the egg rolls soon, plus a surprise."

"Surprise? We'll be waiting. But you'd better hurry. Kimmy overheard me mention Chinese egg rolls, and she's dancing around the room."

"What about you?"

"I'm not dancing, but I'm looking forward to the surprise and to seeing you. We're both anxious."

"Maybe twenty minutes." He ended the call and cringed. His surprise comment sounded like something extraordinary. All he had in mind was a couple of their favorite entrées. He shook his head, frustrated with his silliness. Her tone had changed as if she expected something really special. Not entrées. Whatever she had in mind, he hoped he wouldn't disappoint her too much.

Nina stared at her phone a moment before slipping it into her pocket. Shocked by her own directness, she steadied and sent up another warning to herself. She knew more about his sister than about him. Why had she admitted that she looked forward to seeing him?

Unable to retract her admission, she stepped around Kimmy and headed for the kitchen. Chinese food didn't take long to prepare, and Doug would be there before she knew it. She opened a cabinet and pulled out three plates and silverware, unsure of what she needed but it gave her a distraction.

"Nina." Kimmy's voice piped into the kitchen from the hallway, and she heard her skipping footfalls as she bounded through the door. "What else is Uncle Doug bringing?"

"Else?" She shook her head. "I don't know. He only mentioned egg rolls."

"That's only a ap-tizer. We like wonton soup and Chicken... I can't remember the name."

She grinned at Kimmy. "That sounds like a lot of food."

"We like it." She spiraled and plopped into a chair. "Uncle Doug will probably bring too much. He always does, and today he'll want to make you happy." She tilted her head. "You know why?"

The child's expression confused her. "Not really."

Kimmy giggled. "Because you make him happy." Her grin sank to a frown. "Did you forget? I told you that he's happier when you're with us."

Nina stopped herself from biting her lip. "I guess you did tell me, but I forgot." Never. She couldn't forget that. She ruffled Kimmy's head and gave her a hug. Kimmy rewarded her with a beaming smile and hopped off the chair. "I'm going to watch for him so I can help him carry in the bags."

"Okay, I'll be right here."

As Kimmy skedaddled through the doorway, Nina sank into the empty chair and caught her breath. She'd warned herself many times to keep her emotions in check, but it seemed she'd lost her ability to hang on to her heart. Kimmy had captured her from day one, and Doug's vulnerability was a close second.

He seemed to approach everything with caution when she first met him though he'd opened up a bit. Still, she had her own barricades too, and she'd tried to grant him the same privacy. Yet being on the other end, she disliked it.

Everything had a good explanation. Doug's life seemed to revolve around Kimmy, his sister and his mother. Everyone but himself. Since they'd met, his reaction mirrored a child finding a new friend or getting a new toy. He had something to entertain him for a change. She didn't have to worry about Doug getting romantic ideas. Neither of them were ready for anything. Now all she had to do was convince her prancing pulse and hitching heart.

"Nina." Kimmy's call jerked her from the chair.

She hurried to the living room. "Is he here already?"

"No. There's a lady coming here."

As the words left Kimmy's mouth, she saw Rema climb the porch step. Curious, she reached the door before she rang the bell. "Hi, Rema. What's up?"

She grinned with a shrug. "Nothing important. I thought I'd stop by and say hello again."

Though poor timing, she wanted to be sociable and pushed open the screen. "Come in. I'm waiting for our dinner to be delivered, but he's not here yet."

Rema stepped inside and spotted Kimmy. "Hi." She gave Kimmy a weak wave. "Isn't this Doug's child…niece. I think that's it."

"He's my uncle." Kimmy studied Rema's face. "Do you know him?"

"Not really. I met him at the street party we had at the beginning of September. I think you were playing with Carly."

Kimmy nodded. "Can I sit on the porch and wait for Uncle Doug?"

"Sure you can." Nina welcomed her request, fearing that Rema might say something about her friendship with Doug or ask questions.

Kimmy bounded to the porch, and Nina turned to her surprise visitor. "Would you like to sit?"

"I know you're busy so I won't stay." She checked the nearest chair and sat. "I hope you're learning your way around the city. I know you're new here."

"I've done quite well. That's what's nice about a small town. I have the city map and it's been helpful."

"And you seem to be very friendly with Doug. I'm sure he knows a lot, too."

"Yes, he's been very helpful. I'm helping him with Kimmy sometimes when he has to work late…like today."

"Ahh. I see." She grinned. "Still, if you need any directions or recommendations, just ask." She looked away and seemed to sink into thought. "I'm not sure how long I'm staying here. Maybe I'll get the house. It's hard to know with a divorce settlement coming up."

"Divorce. I'm so sorry." Her lungs depleted for a second, thinking of her own trials. "If you need any advice on that, I've been through one. Not pretty and not what I wanted."

Rema perked up. "Me, either. Far from it. I was blind to Trey's unfaithfulness much longer than I should have been."

Rema's eyes searched hers. "That must have hurt."

"Very. Plus I felt stupid. Then your divorce wasn't because of cheating?"

She drew back a moment, looking for words to explain but said nothing. "No, not that kind of unfaithful…" The statement made no sense to her so Rema couldn't possibly understand what she meant.

"People can be unfaithful in many ways. Dreams they ignore. Promises they don't keep."

Her eyes widened. "You understand. I thought I'd spoken in circles."

"No. I don't suppose you want to talk about

it?" A frown rose on her face. "Sorry, I shouldn't have asked that question."

Though she might be able to trust Rema, she couldn't. She hadn't trusted anyone except Angie, and she hoped that Angie could keep that between the two of them. She wanted no one's pity for being childless. "You're right. He broke the basic promises of the marriage vows to love in sickness and health and in time of trouble. When that happens, doubt and questions smother the love that had been there. They're emotions I don't want to relive."

Rema rose and rested her hand on Nina's shoulder. "I don't want you to relive any of it. I've been struggling with the same. You have a friend who understands." She gave her a pat and stepped away. "Doug will be here soon so I'll say goodbye. Remember if you need anything just ask."

"Thanks. I appreciate your stopping by."

"I enjoyed it." She gave a wave and stepped outside.

Nina returned to the kitchen and grasped the teakettle. She could make decaf coffee, but tea seemed more appropriate for a Chinese dinner. She turned on the burner so it would be ready and placed a glass on the table for Kimmy's milk.

Finished with all she could do until he arrived, she strode back to the living room, and as she entered, Kimmy let out a yell. "He's here."

Nina spun around and hurried toward the door

but Kimmy swung it open, and jiggled behind the screen as Doug appeared on the porch. A strong cold wind followed Doug into the living room.

"It's getting nippy out there." He approached her carrying a large bag and wearing a broad smile. "We won't go hungry."

Nina shook her head. "Should I call around and invite the neighbors?"

Doug winked. "We look forward to leftovers." He turned his head toward Kimmy. "Don't we?"

She dragged her tongue over her lips and nodded.

Still astonished at the size of the sack, Nina reached toward it, but he gave a quick head shake. "I'm fine. Just point the way."

She motioned toward the kitchen and swung ahead of him, knowing she needed more dinnerware. She stood at the counter, watching him unload the containers and trying to keep her reaction to a minimum. Finally she gave up and laughed.

"Chinese has a lot to offer." He lifted the boxes and listed the contents. "Egg rolls, wonton soup, fried rice, pepper steak, chicken with Chinese vegetables, almond cookies and fortune cookies."

Nina turned around to hide her grin as she drew out soup bowls and small plates. Not only from the amount of food but from the joy on his face. Today, Doug's quiet demeanor had blossomed, and she loved it. Her spirit lifted, observing his reaction to something as simple as setting out the multitude of cartons.

She placed the dishes on the table, and then returned for soup spoons and large serving spoons. Finally they gathered around the table, and as she opened her mouth to speak, Kimmy folded her hands and bowed her head while Doug followed. Closing her mouth, she waited and listened to Kimmy's little prayer.

"Come, Lord Jesus, be our guest and let these gifts to us be blessed. Amen."

Doug joined in the *amen*, and she sat in silence, wanting to say it, too, but it felt too strange. She had no idea if God wanted to hear an *amen* from someone who had drifted so far away from Him.

When she lifted her head, Doug's eyes were on her, a look of curiosity on his face. "Are you all right?"

This time she did bite the edge of her lip before managing to speak. "Thank you, Kimmy, for the prayer."

The child gave her a fleeting smile and plucked an egg roll from the container with her fork.

She and Doug chuckled, and the tension faded.

Digging into the excellent food, everyone was silent, even Kimmy, which was rare. Nina grinned to herself, realizing how the presence of a child had changed her life. The child and Doug. She drew in a breath, and Doug gave her another questioning look. She shrugged and monitored her emotional reaction to curb any more conversation.

Kimmy finished first and she asked to be excused. With Doug's approval, she skipped off to the living room, anxious to watch a children's program on TV. They continued in silence for a few moments until Nina stood and gathered the plates and silverware she and Kimmy had used. When she set them on the counter and turned, Doug grinned and laid his fork on his plate.

"I'd better stop or I'll burst."

She flashed him a silly grin. "I wondered." She waved her hand over the abundance left. "Now you can call in the neighbors."

"Leftovers. Did you forget?" He leaned back, his grin still there as if he had to force it.

She shook her head and reached to gather the rest of the dishes.

"Not so fast." He grasped the last small bag. "Dessert, but first…" He motioned for her to sit.

She sank into the chair, curious about his forced grin. "Something's wrong? Is it Roseanne?"

"No. And nothing's wrong. I wanted to tell you that last night after I left here I ran into Angie in front of her house."

Angie? She studied his face, her mind at a standstill.

"She mentioned the wedding, which is coming up fast, and told me you were coming without an escort and she extended an invitation, suggesting I invite you to go with me."

Unable to control her irritation, heat burned on her cheeks. She shook her head. "I'm sorry, Doug. That's no way to be invited to a wedding, and I've already told her that going alone was fine with me, so please don't—"

"Nina, don't apologize. You know Angie. She likes to solve everyone's dilemmas. Apparently she wouldn't want to attend a wedding alone, and she's projecting that on you."

He was right. Angie wanted to fix everything. Even things that didn't need fixing. A burst of air escaped her lungs and she shook her head. "Let's start again, okay?"

He drew back, confusion on his face. "Okay."

The response rang as a question. "The more I thought about going alone I realized it wasn't the best idea, but I'm not seeing anyone right now..." She noticed his expression and grinned. "Naturally I see you, but I meant I'm not dating anyone." She gnawed her lip. "But today when you said you owed me one and said I could ask for anything...the wedding came to mind. I considered asking you to be my escort but I feared I wouldn't have the nerve. So I guess Angie at least opened the door to that."

The tension on his face was replaced by a smile. "She did, it seems. And to answer your question, I would be happy to be your escort. I haven't been to a wedding in years."

His response seemed too easy, yet her shoulders relaxed as she heard the positive tone of his voice. "What about Kimmy?"

His smile broadened. "Angie solved that situation, too. She has someone sitting with Carly and said the girls would have fun together."

"You are kidding." She rolled her eyes, hearing Angie's voice ring in her head.

"Nope. Problem solved." He lifted the smaller bag and set it in front of him. "Now dessert. But we'll have to call Kimmy. She loves fortune cookies."

With his call, Kimmy darted into the room and spotted the crescent treats. "Can I read mine?"

Doug handed her a cookie. She broke it open and tugged out the little slip of paper. She studied it. "'Learning is a tre…'" She held the paper toward Nina. "What's that word?"

"Treasure. Sound it out. Trea-sure."

Kimmy nodded. "'Learning is a treasure that will follow its…owner.' I don't understand."

When she hesitated, Nina eyed the paper. "It means that what you learn will be with you and follow you everywhere."

Kimmy crinkled her nose. "How can learning follow me?"

Nina tousled her hair. "Everything you learn is inside your head so where you go it goes."

She tittered. "My head holds everything."

"Right, my girl." Doug eyed Nina and flagged his little white flag of paper. "Mine says, 'Your home will find happiness.'" He gave her a wink. "That's something I can use."

"Me, too." She lifted the fortune cookie and snapped it open. When she eyed the few words, her chest contracted as the words swam in her head.

Doug cocked his head. "What does it say? We all read ours aloud."

She managed to grin and lifted the ribbon of paper. "'Look around. Your life is changing.'" When she looked at him, her pulse hitched. "Summer's nearly gone and autumn is closing in. Life is changing."

His eyes searched hers as a coy grin slipped to his lips. "Hmm? That's true, but it says your life not the seasons."

Heat crept up her neck. She didn't believe in fortunes. So why had her heart danced? Nothing made sense anymore.

Chapter Five

Doug leaned back against the kitchen chair and savored his coffee. Saturdays always cheered him. Kimmy, to his surprise, had settled on the sofa watching a kids' TV show. Though rare, he liked the moments when he didn't feel the need to entertain her. He'd be a poor father. His knowledge of kids sank in his mind like quicksand. From one day to the next, he tried to recall what necessities were essential for a little girl's needs. If she'd been a boy, he might have a better grasp. He gave five stars to women who seemed to be born with a maternal instinct.

Nina's image formed in his mind, and with her face in his thoughts, he steeled his determination to escort her to Angie's wedding. Though she was irked, an emotion he'd seen before, she admitted she'd planned to ask him. They had both needed the gumption to do it, and he was glad he'd been the one.

The jingle of his cell phone broke through his thoughts, and he grasped it from the table and clicked Talk.

"Are you busy?" Nina's sweet voice sailed from the line.

He eyed his coffee. "Not busy at all. Do you need help?"

"Not from you really, but I promised Kimmy she could help me plant the fall flowers I bought yesterday. Did she tell you?"

"No. She was too wound up about the pinecones and Christmas ornaments."

"I felt bad about that, Doug. She may not be with you at Christmas, but she really wants to make decorations."

Her comment sank into his chest, causing an ache. "I am anxious for Kimmy to be with Roseanne, but it's a change. I'll miss her. Even though life's more complicated with her here, I've begun to breathe it now. I hope you understand what I mean."

"I do. She's important to both of us. She's brought fun and excitement into my humdrum life."

He closed his eyes and pressed his lips together. "Kids are infectious, aren't they?"

Nina chuckled. "You make them sound like a disease."

"A disease of the heart." Burdened with emotion, he segued from his dilemma. "Kimmy's watching TV, but I'm sure she'd prefer to be out-side with you. I'll let her know you're ready for her help."

"Thanks, but only if she wants to. Okay?"

"Sure thing." He ended the call and poured his cooling coffee into the sink. "Kimmy." He strode into the living room as she jumped up from the sofa.

"Are we going to do something?"

"You are." He grinned at her quizzical expres-sion. "Nina's ready to plant flowers."

"Yeah." She clapped her hands but faltered as she looked down at her clothes. "Will I get dirty?"

"Maybe, but everything's washable. Even you."

She giggled as she ran to the door. "I'll see you later, Uncle Doug." She gave a little wave and headed outside.

He watched her through the window, skipping along the sidewalk as if on her way to a party.

Watching her go took him back to the days be-fore Roseanne's accident when he lived a quiet undisturbed life. That time seemed empty now as he pictured his weeks—months—with Kimmy filling the house with giggles and noise. When she vanished beyond his view, loneliness washed over him.

Nina slipped her cell phone into her pocket and headed for the garage, but its ringtone caused her to dig it back out. She hit Talk.

"Nina, how are you, dear? You haven't called in ages."

Her mother rarely called. "Just busy. Is everything okay?"

"I'm fine, dear, and so is your stepdad."

Howard. No matter how hard she tried he had never gained her favor, but she'd made the best of it. The call had a purpose, she knew. "Glad to hear everyone's well." She retreated to the front of the house and pointed to the phone as Kimmy arrived. "Mom, I was getting ready to plant a few perennials so they'll bloom next year. I can't seem to find time during the week." Hoping her mother would get the hint. she waited for her goodbye.

"Flowers for your new house. How nice. And that's somewhat why I'm calling. We thought we might come to visit for Thanksgiving. Wouldn't that be nice?"

Her eyes widened. Nice? Images of Thanksgiving with Doug had entered her thoughts, and hopefully with Kimmy. Now the idea dangled like a loose thread. Her chest tightened. "Yes, it would be nice. But isn't it a long drive and what about bad weather? The north has early snowfalls sometimes. Are you sure Thanksgiving's a good time?"

"We'll fly from Florida and rent a car. That would be easier, we thought."

"Rent a car. Yes, that's good idea."

Kimmy sidled closer. "Are you talking to Uncle Doug?" Her piping voice broke the quiet.

Nina shook her head. "My mother." She'd tried to whisper but it hadn't worked.

"Do you have company, dear?"

"Kimmy just came over to help me with the planting. She's seven and in the second grade."

"Seven? Why in the world are you entertaining a seven-year-old?"

"She entertains me, Mom." She gave Kimmy a wink. "Children like to learn things, and I'm teaching her how to plant flowers."

"Couldn't she learn that from her mother?"

Nina released a stream of air. "Her mother was in a serious accident and she's staying with her uncle, who's a neighbor."

Her mother offered a loud sigh. "I suppose it's none of my business."

That's right, Mom. She muzzled her thought. "Once you make plans about visiting, call and give me the details so I know when to expect you. Okay?"

"I'll call when I know."

Nina held her breath, knowing if she remained silent her mother might catch on.

"Okay, dear. We'll talk later then." Her mother added her goodbye and hung up.

With her mother's visit clinging to her thoughts, she caught her breath. Under normal circumstances, she would be happy for a short visit with her mother. One thing they'd both learned over the years was their personalities tended to clash, and absence didn't always make the heart grow fonder. "What did your mommy want?"

Nina grinned at her curious expression. "She wants to visit for Thanksgiving."

Kimmy smiled. "That will be fun. I hope my mommy can be with us on Thanksgiving, too. I hope she's better."

"I do, too, sweetheart." She wrapped her arm around Kimmy's shoulder. "Are you ready for planting?"

"I'm ready. Then I can tell Carly that I planted flowers, too."

"Maybe she'll see you when we put the ones in the front yard."

She nodded with abandon. "Okay, but what should I do?"

"Let me show you." She guided her to the garage and pushed the button to open the big double door. It slid up, and she steered Kimmy to the plants. "We'll set these out where we want to plant them first."

Kimmy grasped a large pot and waited by the door. Nina hoisted two into her arms and headed out to the front flower beds with Kimmy following. "We'll plant a coneflower on this side and the other over there." Kimmy followed directions and placed the pot where she'd pointed. They added two more plants to the front and then moved to the back after she entered the garage and brought out two trowels, garden gloves, a hand cultivator and a bag of mulch.

In the backyard, she showed Kimmy how to use a trowel to dig the hole and the cultivator to loosen the soil. Once she placed the plant in the hole, Kimmy replaced the dirt and patted it down. Then Nina grabbed the mulch.

"What's that stuff for?" With her nose curled, Kimmy eyed the mixture of soil and compost.

"It insulates the flowers from the winter weather. It protects them."

Her expression changed with the information. "It's good to protect things."

"It is, Kimmy." Her heart constricted. Doug had become Kimmy's protector during the difficult time of her mother's accident. His generous nature and kindness stood out in her mind as a badge of honor. Doug tried to hide those attributes but he'd failed, and in Kimmy's eyes he was a hero. In her eyes, too.

With the planting completed in the back, she and Kimmy carried the gardening tools into the front yard to finish the four plants she'd set in the beds. Before the first plant was done, Nina sensed someone watching and she turned.

Doug stood back, a loving look on his face that sent her pulse skipping. "Spying on our handiwork?"

"Only curious." He ambled toward her and

stood closer to Kimmy as pride glowed on his face. "You have a pretty good helper here, Nina."

"I do. She's a fast learner."

Kimmy gazed at her with her trowel poised in midair. "Tell Uncle Doug about your mommy."

Her grimace managed to become a grin. Mommy? Her mother had never been the mommy type. "My mother called a short time ago. She and my stepfather, Howard, want to visit me here for Thanksgiving. Mother wants to see the house and offer her opinion, I'm sure." The words were out before she could stop them.

Doug gave her a questioning look. "You've never mentioned your mother before."

"I was closer to my dad. My mother and I have a few personality clashes." She winced, unable to admit how much worse it seemed than a few disagreements.

"That can happen. And you have a stepfather."

Her chest tightened. "Daddy died about seven years ago. Mom didn't like living alone."

Curiosity remained on his face, but he didn't ask. Relief eased her nerves. "The good news is we're almost finished here."

"You are?" His spirit had brightened. "That's great, because I have an idea." He gave Kimmy a wink.

"What?" Kimmy paused on her final plant. "Is it fun?"

"I think so. Would you like to go to the Autumn Festival in Durand?"

Kimmy pushed the last pile of soil back into the hole and leaped up, forgetting about the mulch. "What's a festival?"

"They have contests for kids and pumpkin decorating. All kinds of things." He drew her into his arm. "I think it would be fun."

"Can Nina come, too?"

He lifted his gaze to her and grinned. "I'd love her to join us." He tousled Kimmy's hair, then shifted his gaze to Nina. "They have arts and crafts."

His eagerness made her chuckle. "Are you trying to tempt me?" His warm smile melted her.

"Naturally. We can stop at McCurdy Park on the way back and check out their Playscape." He refocused on Kimmy. "I don't think we've been there, have we?"

She shook her head.

"It has swings, slides, rock climbing and bridges for kids."

Kimmy bounced on her heels. "Can we go?"

"What do you say, Nina?"

His eyes captured hers, and she lost her voice for a moment. "Sounds…like fun. Right, Kimmy?"

Kimmy gave a vigorous nod.

Doug sidled to her. "Okay, when you're ready we'll leave."

"As soon as I add the mulch we're finished." She bent down and emptied some compost on the plant.

"While you finish there, I'll run home and let Kimmy get cleaned up. I'll be back to get you in a few minutes."

She eyed her dirty pants and dirt-streaked arms. "Make that twenty minutes." She rose and showed him her dirt-speckled skin.

"Half hour." He gave her a smile and turned toward home with Kimmy skipping beside him.

Doug eased into his recliner as Kimmy skipped off to wash and change. His mind turned to its new favorite subject. Nina. His thoughts fluttered from trying to guess her feelings for him to trying to decipher his own. He liked her. Liked her a lot, but he had so much on his plate with little to offer a woman.

Maybe worse was Nina's protected past life. She divulged so little, even regarding her mother. What had happened? He had learned nothing about her mother except their personality differences, and he suspected the problem was deeper than that. He saw it in her expression, but Nina monitored what she told him. Only when she was willing to give could he weigh the possibility of something greater.

Yet no matter what his reservations told him, he still admired her generosity and her open heart that welcomed Kimmy into her life while he dragged along behind. He knew she'd been married once, so why no children? Had her husband not wanted them? He had no doubt Nina would welcome a child with her arms and heart wide-open.

"Ready." Kimmy's excited voice entered the room before she did.

When she came through the doorway, he was pleased to see her face shiny clean and her clothes ready for fun. She already had an eye for color. He grinned, thinking of the times he'd struggled to match pants and shirt or suit with a suitable tie.

He checked his watch. "We should give Nina a few more minutes. Do you want a snack?"

"Can't we eat at the place we're going?" She ran her tongue over her lips. "Like a hot dog?"

"What if they don't have food?"

She plunked her fists against her waist and leaned forward, eye to eye. "Uncle Doug, who doesn't have food?"

He arched a brow. "Okay. We'll look for a hot dog." He drew her into his arms and she slipped onto his lap. "We could call your mom and see how she's doing. What do you say?"

"I say yes…but can we still go to the slides and other places?"

"For sure." He reached into his shirt pocket and pulled out his phone. Roseanne's phone rang and when he'd just about given up, he heard the click. "Roseanne?"

"Sorry, Doug, my doctor stopped in and was saying goodbye when the phone rang. I couldn't find it in the bedclothes." She chuckled. "Is everything okay?"

"That's what I called to ask you. Kimmy hasn't talked to you in a while so before we go out for the day, I thought we'd call. Here she is." He handed her the phone and watched her face light up when she heard her mother's voice.

"Mommy, are you better now?"

She listened, her questioning frown lessening with every word. "Really? Then I can see you sometimes."

His curiosity amplified the frown on his face. "Kimmy, let me talk before you hang up."

She nodded. "We're going to a place with contests for kids and all kinds of fun things and then to the swings and slides."

He waited until she reiterated all he'd said to her, and he hoped the festival was as much fun as she envisioned it. He kept his guard up, fearing she might forget and click off the conversation.

"Uncle Doug wants to talk, Mommy." She returned the phone with a broad smile. "Mommy has a surprise."

Being released? The possibility divided his emotions. "Roseanne, what's up?"

"They're moving me to a rehabilitation center

close to home, Doug. When I can handle things without too much assistance, I'll finish any other therapy at home. It won't be long now, and I'll at least be close to you so I can see Kimmy more easily. You won't have to make those horribly long trips. I know that's been difficult."

"Great news. I wish you could see Kimmy's face. But I need to be honest. I'm going to miss her. The house will be too quiet when she returns home."

"Doug, I know you don't want to hear this, but you need to get serious about your life. You've put all your energy into your work and nothing into relationships. I hope my bad relationships haven't influenced you. I'd feel—"

"Roseanne, you know better than that. I was shy in high school. Mom and Dad had a relationship that seemed practical. I never saw much romance there, and I don't think most women want to get involved for companionship alone. I didn't think I had much more to offer."

"Don't use other people's lives to build your own, Doug. You've been such a great brother to me. You've always been there for me and now for Kimmy. I can't tell you how much I appreciate that, but life is wonderful when you have the right person. I'm still trying. You know that. Kimmy is the love of my life, but I also want some romance and intimacy. My sweet daughter can't provide that for me or for you."

"Thanks for your concern, Roseanne, but I'm a big boy and I'm learning. In fact, I have to pick up Nina. She's going with us."

"That doesn't help if she's a friend of Kimmy's."

"She's my friend, too. Nina's a neighbor who has kindly watched Kimmy for me a few times, and yes, she's single. Divorced to be exact."

"Single. That's a step in the right direction, dear brother. Now I can breathe a little easier." She chuckled. "I'm doing well, Doug. Painful therapy and it's frustrating trying to get around, but I'm doing better. That's progress."

"It's great news, Roseanne. We have to get going, but lots of love from me and Kimmy."

Kimmy leaned into the phone. "I love you, Mommy."

He held the phone to her ear. "I love you with all my heart, Kimmy. It won't be long, sweetie."

"I know." She beamed and stepped away.

Doug ended the conversation, his spirit rising for Kimmy. He slipped the cell phone into his pocket, and they were on their way.

Kimmy pulled a hunk of cotton candy from the cone. Nina chuckled, watching the floss melt on her tongue. She knew that Kimmy ate healthy food with no qualms, so she muted her thoughts about the sugar.

"Want some?" Kimmy held the fluffy cone toward her.

"No, thank you. The hot dog filled me, and I smell popcorn coming from somewhere. Before we leave, I might get some of that." Free popcorn, cotton candy, coffee. A generous festival and a great idea to create community spirit.

Doug caught her arm. "Look over there." He pointed to a man holding a chain saw. "The man is making things with that saw."

His eyes bright with interest, she and Kimmy followed him to the barricaded area. Amazed at the man's talent, she watched the chain saw artist create part of a bench with birds providing the legs on each side of the seat. Earlier they'd admired sidewalk chalk artists and laughed at the decorated pumpkin display.

She'd eyed the arts and crafts but couldn't decide on anything. Kimmy had also passed on the children's games. Other than watching a clown make balloon animals and having a small butterfly painted on her cheek, Kimmy had only watched.

Fearing the event had been a disappointment to her, she sidled closer to Doug. "Should we see if Kimmy would rather go to the Playscape?"

He gave her a wink and introduced the idea to Kimmy. Her rousing *let's go* made their decision.

Though she'd enjoyed spending time with both Kimmy and Doug, Nina's spirit had been dented by the news that Roseanne was being transferred closer to home and would be released soon. Her selfish attitude struck a bad chord, but she faced that life would change for her and Doug when Kimmy was gone. Kimmy had been the catalyst for much of their time together. The upcoming wedding might be the only event they would share alone. With Kimmy back with her mother, life would slip back into the occasional contact with neighbors and her work. Not much to say for that.

Doug had brought a new spirit to her life, one that caused her to anticipate the day. She looked forward to waking in the morning to see what the day held. But all of their activities had Kimmy as their focus. They would be at a loss without her.

Doug steered them away from the festival to his car, and they slipped in and headed back to Corunna and McCurdy Park, less than ten miles away. Doug parked as close as he could to the Playscape and Kimmy unsnapped her seat belt and darted across the grass before they closed their doors.

Nina grinned at Kimmy's exuberance. "This is more like it, I think."

He gave a nod. "I suspected she'd love this, but she wouldn't have gotten her sugar quota for the day without the cotton candy." He chuckled. "Hopefully she'll burn off the energy here."

She moved to his side and they followed Kimmy's path to the tower of play equipment. The late-summer sun spread across her shoulders, and she enjoyed it, knowing that soon a cold wind would replace the warm rays. The idea filtered through her mind. Life was like that, too.

Doug's arm shifted beside hers, brushing against her and warming her thoughts. When they were together, her emptiness seemed to be a thing of the past. Yet reality sat on her doorstep, waiting for the door to close and lock her inside again. Caught up in the moment, she took a step and stumbled. As she hurled forward, Doug caught her in his arms and drew her up as if she weighed nothing. With his arms around her, his eyes met hers. "Careful. Those sneaky sticks are out to get you."

She grinned, adhered to his gaze, her lungs begging for breath with his lips so close she could almost feel them on hers. She grasped her wits and dragged her eyes from his. "Thanks for the save."

"We Boy Scouts promise to be prepared."

"Were you really a Boy Scout?"

"No, but I had friends who were. Nothing wrong with helping a woman in distress." He ran his hand down her arm and wove his fingers through hers. "For safety." He lifted their knitted fingers. "Okay?"

"Thanks." She managed the comment, uncomfortable with her giddy feeling. Based on her reaction to hand-holding, she might drop over dead if he kissed her. Heat rose in her chest and she worked to keep it from cresting.

The ground evened out as they neared the Playscape, yet his fingers remained woven with hers. When they reached a bench, he motioned for her to sit. Through the slats of the play area, they could see Kimmy climb the tower and zoom down the tube slide to the ground. Without seeing them, she made her way back up the tower.

Doug slipped his arm along the back of the bench, his body close to hers. "Nina, I'm having a difficult time."

Her heart jumped with his confession.

"I am thrilled that Roseanne is being transferred closer, but I know what that means."

While wrangling her disappointment that she'd misconstrued his confession, she understood, having dealt with the same feelings. "It will be different, Doug. Quieter."

"Lonelier." He shook his head. "She's forced me to come out of my shell—a shell I don't totally understand, but one I've lived with—and I'm afraid I'll slide back into my reclusive world. Work, home and church. That's what it's been. Not much social life." He shook his head. "I don't want to be there again."

"You don't have to, Doug. No one put you there but you, and you have the power to live outside those narrow walls."

"I know."

His head lowered and he fell deep in thought, thought she didn't feel right to disturb.

Finally he looked up. "I know I should be in control, but my mind goes blank. Without Kimmy to stimulate action, it's easy to sit in a chair and stare at TV programs I don't care about or read a book that my heart isn't in."

"Maybe you're reading the wrong book." She hoped it sounded lighthearted, but he didn't laugh and she wanted to apologize. "Seriously, Doug. Look around. What do people do? Get involved in church activities. I'm sure they have programs that need volunteers. Most organizations do. Become a Big Brother. Have you thought about that?"

He shook his head. "I don't have much to offer kids. You see how I stumble around with Kimmy. If it weren't for you, I'd be telling her to read a book or do her puzzles, about the same as her mother does."

"That's not true. And since she's been here, you've discovered all kinds of good activities for kids. What about the train museum for a boy? Don't they let kids get inside during the train festival? And this Playscape. Boys would like this. Take a boy to a sporting event. Most kids would love that."

His eyes searched hers. "You have the ideas."

"So would you if you didn't doubt yourself."

She laid her hand on his. "Doug, you've set your mind on being a failure. I don't know why, and I'm not sure you know either, but it's not really who you are. I see your delight with Kimmy. Yes, she's your niece, but a boy who needs a male friend can be a delight, too. You can teach him how to catch a ball, how to play croquet or badminton. Those are things you can purchase in most toy stores. Or get yourself a dog. They can be the best company and they're faithful."

Her voice had betrayed her. From his expression, he'd caught her tone on the faithful comment, an emphasis she'd hoped to control. Her mind shot to Rema's surprise visit and the discussion they'd had on faithfulness.

"Uncle Doug, did you see me?" Kimmy's voice severed their silence.

"We saw you on the big slide." He nodded.

Kimmy's face made it clear she meant something else. "Not that. I walked on the swinging bridge and I climbed on the caterpillar." She pointed away from the wooden structure. "Over there."

Doug glanced at her, surprise on his face. "I didn't see you over there."

Nina hadn't seen a thing but Doug's expression as they talked. He shorted himself so much when it came to children. His confidence at work seemed opposite to his uncertainty with children.

The discrepancy aroused questions, but those would have to wait.

Doug rose. "Are you ready to go?"

"If you come and see me on the caterpillar." She beckoned him to follow.

Nina stood and treaded along the path to the freestanding metal structure with the look of a crawling caterpillar, its back humped as it moved forward. Kimmy straddled the red metal tail and used the rungs to work her way up the high hump, then wiggled around to climb down the hump before she grasped the final rung to reach the insect's bright blue head and yellow antennae.

They applauded as she grinned and lifted her hand as if she'd conquered Mount Everest. "Good job, Kimmy." Doug reached her side and helped her jump from the metal structure.

Nina slipped her arm around Kimmy. "If I were littler, I'd climb it, too."

"You can do it." Kimmy's eyes brightened, and Nina, wishing she'd not offered the suggestion, shook her head.

"No. You're too good."

Perfect response. Kimmy gave an agreeing nod and skipped along beside them as they wended their way back to the car.

Nina's spirit lifted, then sank as Roseanne's news struck her again. One day Kimmy would be back with her mother, a wonderful gift really. But for Doug and her, it would change the course of their lives. Did it have to? Couldn't they continue to be friends and enjoy each other's company? Doug had made no overtures for anything beyond friendship. Even holding her hand earlier had been out of concern that she might fall again. That was all it had been.

The recollection of his firm grip revived the warm feeling she'd experienced, a sense of security she'd had only rarely in her life when she was young and her father took her places. The loss of a relationship with Doug would be another loss even greater than her divorce. Before marriage, Todd had seemed to be a kind man. He had a good job and had been generous, but the intimacy she'd expected from their marriage had faded quickly. It died after she'd lost the second child. Died as quickly as their marriage.

Doug faltered at the car and gave her a questioning look. She smiled back, unwilling to talk about Kimmy returning to her mother's home and what that meant to them. She would wait and see. That's all she could do.

Chapter Six

Doug stood in Roseanne's doorway while Kimmy stood beside him, studying her mother, who seemed to be asleep. Her transfer had occurred sooner than he expected, and he struggled with pangs of selfish sorrow. Soon Roseanne would be home. He'd always adored Kimmy, but since she'd been with him so long, he'd grown even fonder of her, far more than he anticipated.

Roseanne stirred and lifted her head. A smile parted her lips, and she opened her arms as Kimmy darted to her bedside. He stayed back, allowing mother and daughter to share the special moment. A month had passed since they had been together. Roseanne had been in pain and didn't want Kimmy to see her during that time. Though they had spoken on the phone, it could never replace being together.

When Roseanne noticed him, she beckoned him inside the room. "Why are you standing back like a stranger.?" She grinned, her arm wrapped around Kimmy as she leaned half-prone on the mattress, her feet dangling toward the floor.

He sauntered closer. "It's called bonding."

She tilted her head. "You're right." She shook her head. "As always, big brother."

"And don't forget it." He grasped the arm of the chair and moved it closer. Then he lifted Kimmy and set her on the edge of the bed. As soon as he did, she leaned her cheek against Roseanne's chest.

"I've had fun with Uncle Doug, Mommy, but I miss you, too." She turned her head to face her mom.

"I'm glad you're having fun. I would be sad if you had a terrible time." She petted Kimmy's cheek. "But I missed you, too."

"You were sick." Kimmy lifted her head and kissed her mother's cheek.

"Very, and you wouldn't have wanted to see me whining."

Kimmy giggled. "Did you really whine?"

"Sometimes." Her eyes shifted to his. "But Uncle Doug will only have to put up with you for a few more weeks. I want to be home by Christmas. Maybe sooner."

"Really?" Kimmy's eyes sparkled as brightly as her smile. "But can we go to see Uncle Doug before Christmas, because I want to make Christmas ornaments."

"Ornaments?" Roseanne drew her head back as if questioning. Kimmy giggled at her curiosity, and she rattled on about making the decorations.

His mind sailed back to Nina and the plans she'd made for the Christmas pinecones. His chest ached not only for his plans but for Nina, who had admitted that her life had been solitary, too, before she'd moved to Lilac Circle—perhaps since her husband left her.

Again the question haunted him. Why? Why had her marriage failed?

While Kimmy and Roseanne talked, he glanced around, looking for flowers or a stack of cards, anything that might have let Roseanne know she was missed. He didn't see much, but the drawer in her stand held get well cards. Flowers seemed a simple gift and they would last after he and Kimmy had gone.

"While you two talk—" he rose "—I'm going for a walk. I'll be back shortly."

Although Roseanne gave him a questioning look, he escaped. He hurried down to the lobby, found the gift store and headed for the floral arrangements behind the window. He spotted one in a white vase filled with colorful flowers in reds, yellow and orange shades. They reminded him of the trees beginning to color. Soon they would be in full autumn hues like fire. He purchased the flowers and a box of chocolate mints. Rose-anne liked those.

When he returned, Kimmy had stretched out beside her, and the first thing he heard was something about Nina. He faltered, wishing he could stand outside the door and listen like an eaves-dropper. Instead he strode in with the bouquet.

A smile lit Roseanne's face. "I wondered where you were sneaking to."

"Sneaking? I said I was going for a walk. I did." He set the flowers on her stand and placed the chocolate mints beside it. "Something for your sweet tooth."

"Doug, you remembered." She raised on her elbow and reached over to grab the box. Before taking her own, she offered one to him, which he declined, and one to Kimmy, bubbling with enthusiasm as she accepted it.

Roseanne popped one in her mouth and arched her eyebrow. "Kimmy was telling me how much fun you both have with Nina."

He released a breath. "I'm not sure I would call it fun, but it's pleasant."

Kimmy rolled over and jammed her fist into her waist. "Uncle Doug, you do too have fun. You laugh a lot when Nina's with us, and you smile more than ever."

He managed not to wince at her honesty. "I'm being amiable."

"What?" Kimmy gave him one of her looks.

"You're being fun and nice. You like Nina, don't you?"

"Yes, I like Nina." A lot, but he avoided admitting it even to himself. "She's very nice, and she really likes you, Kimmy."

"She really likes you, Uncle Doug. She told me."

He wanted to control his surprise, but he felt his jaw drop so it was too late. "I'd better stop going for walks. All kinds of things happen."

Roseanne shook her head. "Doug, I've said it over and over. Life is out there waiting to happen. Don't lose something or someone that could make a huge difference in your life."

Though Nina filled his thoughts, Kimmy also fit the description. He kept his mouth shut. "I'll heed your warning, sis."

Kimmy gave him a bigger frown, probably lost in the meaning of *heed*.

A sound behind him gave him pause. Before he turned, Roseanne acknowledged the visitor. "That time already?" She shook her head. "More therapy. It never ends."

"But it's what's needed for you to go home and be on your own again." He rose and shifted back his chair. "Kimmy, I think our visit has to end so your mom can have her therapy."

Kimmy slipped from the bed. "I want you to get better, Mommy, so you try hard to walk and stuff, okay?"

Roseanne pulled her closer and kissed her. "Okay, and it won't be long. Since I'm closer, you can come and visit me again."

"I will. Uncle Doug said we can come more often."

"And bring Nina. I'd like to meet her."

"Okay!" She bounded from the bed her face beaming. "I'll tell her you want to meet her, okay?"

"Okay." Roseanne gave a wave as they moved out of the way for the empty wheelchair. With one more goodbye, he steered Kimmy into the corridor, longing to ask her how much she told Roseanne. Instead, he let well enough alone. Maybe later he could think of a subtle way to ask. Kimmy was too smart for her age.

A nippy breeze penetrated Nina's jacket as she treaded along the sidewalk to El's. She hadn't talked to him in a couple of weeks, and when she pulled the batch of cookies from the oven, he broke through her thoughts. She'd decided to make Snickerdoodles with the wonderful texture that cream of tartar seemed to add. She'd sneaked one herself.

Approaching El's home without him in the yard looked strange, but the weather had curtailed that. Indian summer had taken a vacation. El's car was in the driveway near the garage so she was reassured that he was home. She climbed the porch steps and rang the bell. In a moment he answered with a smile so bright it warmed her.

"How nice." He pushed open the door. "And I see you're bearing a gift." His eyes twinkled as they did when he suspected she'd brought him a sweet treat.

She handed him the bag and followed him inside, but when she saw the dining room, her pulse skipped and she drew back. "Birdie." She moved forward, following El's beckoning. "How nice to see you."

She grinned, and seeing Birdie smile was a bigger surprise. "El and I are just visiting. It's too cold to do much outside."

Nina agreed and sank into the chair beside her.

"El, bring Nina a cup of coffee." Birdie turned to face her. "Or do you prefer tea?"

"Either is fine, but—"

"Coffee with cream. It's on the table." El ambled into the room carrying a mug, the steam rising, and a plate of the cookies. "Now, this is a nice addition, Birdie."

Birdie eyed the treat and accepted the plate. She took one and passed it to Nina.

"I already had one at home." Nina set the plate close to El, noticing some crumbs on his lips so she was assured he'd already tried them. "I was thinking about the weather on the way here. I hope it warms up for the wedding or at least it's a sunny day."

"No matter what the weather, Angie and Rick will have sunshine in their hearts." El gave her a wink.

"You're right." Her wedding had filled her mind and heart with joy and hope for an amazing future. But as marriage did sometimes, her sunshine turned to gloom.

"Angie said you were invited, too." He grasped another cookie and took a bite.

"Yes, I was surprised."

He frowned, and then seemed to understand. "New to the neighborhood, but when Angie connects with someone, she's a faithful friend. I've noticed that. She's been good to me."

"Me, too." Birdie shook her head. "And I didn't deserve it."

El waved his hand through the air. "Birdie, everyone deserves friendship. You made a few mistakes, but now you let your personality break free from that negativity." He rested his hand on her shoulder. "When I told Angie you were my date for the wedding, she was happy. Really happy. I saw it on her face."

Nina guessed Angie had set that one up, too.

"You're not going alone, are you, Nina?" El's eyes glinted.

She suspected he already knew the answer, and she grinned. "You know I'm not."

"Last I heard you were going alone, but I'd hoped—"

"You hoped Angie's meddling would work, and it did."

His expression gave him away. "And I'm glad, Nina."

"Angie loves to play matchmaker, but I'd already considered asking Doug." Surprised at her admission, she swallowed and decided to hush up. She trusted El, but Birdie had been the street gossip, which still left her uncertain.

Birdie gave a nod. "You two have become good friends and I see that little girl—what's her name—is fond of you."

"Kimmy. I'm fond of her, too. She and Doug are visiting her mother today. She's been transferred to a rehabilitation facility that's much closer, and she should be home soon."

"In time for Christmas. That's wonderful." El faltered as a frown appeared. "But that means both you and Doug will miss her."

"Very much. I feel selfish that I want something to happen so Kimmy stays, and I feel terrible when it enters my mind."

"Oh, the Lord understands what emotions love can bring out of us, Nina. Don't fret. He forgives before we ask. God is love and He made us in His image."

Her admission lightened her, and her shoulders straightened. "Thank you, El. I forget so many things about God's blessings."

"We all fall short of God's commandments and

desires for us. I'm sure that's why He gave us the forgiveness that comes through Jesus."

Forgiveness brought up another topic she'd had in mind when she brought the cookies over, but today she eyed Birdie and hesitated.

"Nina, you have something else on your mind, don't you?"

El's uncanny ability threw her off balance for a moment. "Speaking of forgiveness, I do have a situation that's troubling me." Though Birdie listened, she told him about her mother and step-father's Thanksgiving visit. "It puts a damper on being thankful, El, and that shames me but it's true. Mother has always been critical. Even if something is nice, she adds a *but* to the sentence. It ruins the compliment or the noncommittal re-action to something."

"Are you thankful for things not related to your mother?" A look in his eyes signaled he'd cornered her.

"You know I am. I'm grateful for meeting my new neighbors and for people like you and Angie who brought me out of myself and into the warmth of new relationships."

"And what about Doug? And Kimmy?"

Her chest exploded with emotion. "Yes, I am very grateful for Doug's friendship and the joy of meeting Kimmy. She's changed my attitude and my life in a way." Her admission shone on her face like a neon advertisement.

"In what way, Nina?" El's forehead crinkled. "Did you have a bad attitude toward children?"

"No. Not at all. I can't—" Unable to go on, she swallowed her words and closed her eyes, willing away the tears that had come without warning.

"Dearest Nina, we are friends who care about you. Please let us help if we can, and if not us, the Lord has promised to take your burdens from you. 'My yoke is easy, and my burden is light.' Those are Jesus's words."

"I'm trying to remember those things, El. I'm trying, but sometimes…"

"Sometimes it's good to say it and then pack it away. You said that you can't—"

He lifted his brows, waiting for her to finish, but the words tangled in her head. When she could stand the silence no longer, she admitted what she could. "I've learned I can never have a child."

"*Never* is a powerful word, Nina."

"But it takes two people with strong love and healthy bodies to bring a child into the world, El, and I realized that Todd and I didn't have the gift of love, and then I—" The admission raked through her being.

"That was one relationship. What about another one? Two people whose love is strong and two people who think of a child as a bonus package of love from the Lord."

She bit her lip. "I never expected to find a relationship that strong, El, and even if I do, it doesn't change the fact that I'm physically unable to carry a child. I'm not sure that I will find a man who has enough love for that."

Though he shook his head, a faint smile curved El's mouth. "But you know a man like that, Nina."

Doug. El's expression gave the answer without question. "Yes, but I don't see our friendship heading in that direction."

Though Birdie had been silent throughout, she released a long sigh. "You're seeing with warped eyes, Nina. Take a fresh look. I never thought my life would change or I would find a person with patience enough to like me as a friend, but look at my life now. El is a man who knows how to bring the best out of people and to make them see that they have better inside. My life is different, and I see things differently. Maybe one day you will, too."

"Very wise, Birdie." El reached across the table and slipped his hand over hers. "I'm proud of you. You said that very well."

Nina hadn't expected to take much stock in anything Birdie said, but at the moment, her attitude had altered. Letting someone bring out the best in her could change how she saw things. Birdie had a point. But how did that happen? She needed to think about it, but she wanted to do that alone.

* * *

"Stop, Uncle Doug!"

Kimmy's voice ripped through Doug's thoughts with a blast. He pulled to the edge of the road and stopped, his heart banging against his chest. "What's wrong? Are you sick?"

She gave him a look as if he was stupid. "No. I thought we would stop at Nina's?"

He shook his head instead of shaking hers. "Kimmy, you scared me nearly to death. Don't do that, okay? I thought something was wrong." He stared at his niece, realizing how her heart had wrapped around Nina's. "Can I park the car at home first?"

"Can I get out?"

"No. It will only take a minute." He'd refused her something, one of his rare moments, but she had to learn that life didn't revolve around her as much as he knew it had for some time. And it wasn't just him. Nina jumped at her commands, too.

Though a wonderful little girl, Kimmy's situation had motivated him and Nina to try to make her life better. She'd done well with her mom's illness, but he needed to get her back to real life. When she returned home to live with her mother again, she wouldn't be the center of attention. Her mother would be, since she still had many needs.

A sigh escaped from his depths. Even thinking about Kimmy leaving ripped through his heart.

He turned off the motor and looked into the backseat. "Now, was that so bad?"

Though she wore a frown, she shook her head and opened the passenger side. "I guess not."

Instead of responding, he remained quiet. He had to be patient with her. Life was changing, and Kimmy was old enough and smart enough to recognize it. As she rounded the car, he met her at the back and put his arm around her shoulders. Without a word, he guided her down the driveway to the sidewalk, heading for Nina's.

He noticed her head shift, and when he looked, she gave him a smile.

Tension lifted from his chest, but he knew the situation had to be addressed. "Are you sad about saying goodbye to your mom again?"

She shrugged. "I miss her, but..." She lowered her head as if counting cracks in the concrete sidewalk.

"But?"

"But I'll miss being here, too. Carly is my new friend and so is Nina. And you are the best uncle in the world."

Though he opened his mouth to speak, emotion lodged in his throat. He gulped down the sob and gave her shoulders a squeeze. "That was a sweet thing to say, Kimmy. You are the best niece in the world, too. I will miss seeing you every day, but I know your real home is with your mom."

"I know."

Her comment reached him as a whisper, and she, too, dealt with the emotion of change. Children also felt the pangs of sorrow and loneliness. As they walked up Nina's sidewalk, he spotted her at the window. She opened the door and held it wide as they entered.

"Did you have a good visit, Kimmy?"

From Nina's expression, she seemed to sense a mood swing in Kimmy, who usually skipped up her driveway. She gave Kimmy a hug and then drew back. "How about some lunch or—"

"We ate after we left the facility. Thanks, though." He gave her a smile and settled into the easy chair she motioned toward. "How was your day?"

"Good. I had a nice visit with El and Birdie. They seem to be quite a couple lately."

"Is that good?" He recalled hearing about the infamous Birdie when he first moved in.

She looked thoughtful a moment. "I think it is. She's not the same Birdie I met when I moved in. She's more positive. She listens, and when she talks, she has something worthwhile to offer rather than the street gossip or her misconstrued situations." She chuckled. "I think she likes herself now."

He loved hearing her voice lilt without the weight of worry.

"Kimmy, tell me about your visit." Nina drew

Kimmy closer and eased her beside her on the sofa. "I bet your mom was happy to see you."

"She was, and you know what Uncle Doug did?"

He drew back, his heart in his throat.

Nina gave her a playful frown. "What?"

"He bought my mom a vase with flowers in it. They were pretty and my mom loved them."

Nina's frown vanished. "I'm sure she did. Every lady I know loves bouquets of flowers. They're bright and cheerful, and they say *I love you.*"

Kimmy giggled. "Flowers don't talk."

"No, but that's what they mean."

Kimmy appeared to toss that around in her head. "Then I would like flowers, too."

"We all do. It's a girl thing."

"And you know what else?" She leaned closer. "My mommy wants you to come and visit her."

Nina's head drew back. "She does. Why?"

She glanced at him, and all he could do was shrug. He'd only caught the end of the conversation when he returned with the flowers.

Kimmy giggled again. "'Cuz I told her that Uncle Doug is happier when he's with you."

Her revelation struck him with the blow of a jackhammer.

Nina glanced his way but without an ounce of surprise on her face, and then he knew. Kimmy had already revealed this to her. No wonder she dropped a barricade between them on occasion. Yet even that thought sent an ache through him. He'd hoped she, at least, enjoyed their friendship. Though needing to respond in some way, he searched his mind and came up empty. How could a person dissuade the honesty of a child?

Kimmy eyed him waiting for something.

He finally grasped a response. "Maybe you make me happy, Kimmy? Is that possible?"

She tittered, her head swaying like a bobblehead. "It's not the same. You look different with Nina. I see those looks on TV."

"You aren't watching adult programs with me, Kimmy."

"I know, but I do at home sometimes when Mom finally takes a break."

This time he became a bobblehead, unable to push away her comment without it bobbing back and making him look a fool. He eyed Nina, who had got quiet since Kimmy's declaration. "I admit I've enjoyed meeting a neighbor who is so kind and a lot of fun. So maybe I am happier."

Kimmy nodded her head. "See, I told you."

Changing the subject was the only way to go. "By the way, I looked at the extended weather forecast. We're supposed to have another break in the weather. I think we'll have a sunny day for Angie's wedding. The temperature is supposed to be back in the midseventies. That should be nice."

"I hope you're right. I've been trying to think

of something to wear, but I guess that's something only girls care about." Still beside her, Nina gave Kimmy a playful poke.

"Can I help you find a dress?" Her eyes brightened as she gazed at Nina.

"Not today since it's getting dark already, but maybe tomorrow. I need to find something soon or I'll have to go shopping."

Kimmy slipped forward on the sofa and clapped her hands. "We can go shopping. Yeah."

He shook his head. "Kimmy, she didn't say anything about *we*."

Her eyes filled with pleading turned to Nina. "Can I?"

"Maybe I own something already, sweetie. We'll see after we look." She turned an arched brow to him. "That's if your uncle Doug doesn't mind."

Angie had mentioned the darkness and she was right. He hadn't noticed. He rose. "If you have to go shopping and want to take this young lady with you, it's fine with me."

"Yeah." She stood and jigged around Nina. "I hope you have to shop."

From Nina's expression, he guessed she didn't, but Kimmy would deal with it.

"We'd better get home. Tomorrow is a school day, and it's time for a young lady to take a bath and think about bedtime."

Kimmy looked around. "What young lady?" Then she giggled.

He slipped his arm around her shoulders. "Good night, Nina. Sleep well."

Kimmy slipped from his arm and hurried over to Nina, drew her down and kissed her cheek. "Good night. I'll see you tomorrow after school."

Doug drew in a deep breath. Tonight had been a revelation. He had no idea what Kimmy had been telling Nina or what she thought about it. He could only pray that Kimmy's prattle hadn't done any damage to the friendship they had cultivated. It still needed a lot of hoeing and maybe a few fresh seeds of hope.

Chapter Seven

Nina plopped on the edge of her mattress, her frustration tightening her shoulders. She had scoured her closet for something special to wear to the wedding and found nothing. Going alone to the wedding she wouldn't have cared, but she had sort of a date.

She caught her image in the vanity mirror and shook her head. Her sort-of-a-date thought had twisted her mouth to a pitiful grin. How could someone have a sort-of date? It either was one or it wasn't one. Since Angie had influenced the situation, she had a difficult time thinking of it as a normal date.

She threw her hands into the air and gave up. Date or no date, she had an escort and wanted to look nice. Doug was good-looking in jeans and a polo shirt. She could only imagine how striking he would be in a suit, his broad shoulders above a trim waist.

The thought rippled down her chest, making her too aware of the growing feelings she could no longer deny. Asking herself what she could do had become pointless. She'd read enough of the Bible to admit that the outcome was not totally in her hands.

She eyed the dark red dress she'd stretched across the chair and curled her nose. The dress didn't suit her, especially since she'd lost a few pounds after she'd moved to Lilac Circle. Life had become more active and filled with toting, flower planting and entertaining Kimmy. The experience had been good for her.

Kimmy would be there for a while longer, and since she could do nothing about her returning home, she'd recognized her useless worrying.

She rose and hung the dress back in the closet, admitting she needed a new dress. That would make Kimmy ecstatic. The image aroused her smile.

Grasping her cell phone, she wandered into the kitchen and sat at the table as she called Doug. When he answered, her pulse skipped as it did each time she heard his voice. "Tell Kimmy the shopping event is on."

"I'm glad to hear it since I heard about nothing else this morning before school. I'll drop her by when I pick her up from school."

"See you then, Doug."

He hung up after telling her he was dealing

with a new client. She understood, having those situations, too. But thankfully so much of her work could be done at home that an episode of impatience was witnessed by no one.

She eyed the clock to validate she had time to put a dent in one more job before Doug dropped off Kimmy. She made a quick mug of her favorite tea and settled in front of the computer. With work her focus, time flew and before she knew it a door slammed outside and she suspected her shopping partner had arrived. She saved the work and rose.

When she reached the living room, she heard Kimmy's piping voice before they rang the bell. She opened the door, and Kimmy's beaming smile warmed her heart. "Come in a minute." When she pushed back the screen door, Kimmy sailed in with Doug in her wake.

Doug gave her one of these eye-roll looks. "Someone's excited."

"I noticed." She slipped her arm around Kimmy's shoulder. "I looked at all my dresses and didn't like any of them for the wedding so… guess who's going to be my helper."

Kimmy poked her finger into her chest. "Me."

"Right." She eyed Doug, waiting with a grin. "Are you coming, too?"

He chuckled. "Not unless you need a man's opinion, and I don't think you do."

"Right again." She managed a lighthearted

smile, but part of her would love to spend more time with him. Obviously this trip wasn't an appropriate time. "I'll get your opinion on Saturday."

He nodded. "I can't wait."

She located her bag and returned. "Ready, Kimmy?"

She rushed to her side. "I'm ready."

Doug headed for the door with Kimmy on his heels, eagerness shining on her face. She locked the door and headed for her car. Doug followed and helped Kimmy buckle her seat belt, then closed her door and watched as she drove away.

When she reached downtown, Nina spotted a couple of consignment shops but decided to keep those for later. Instead she drove to a store she knew had numerous choices of women's evening wear. Kimmy jiggled in the backseat ready to make her escape, and when they finally reached the parking lot, she charged from the car and waited for Nina to round the car and meet her.

Inside, she headed for the women's department and then for the dresses. Kimmy began pointing to dresses before she could get a good look. "Hang on and let me find my size."

"But Uncle Doug said you would look pretty in purple and this one is purple, isn't it?"

Her chest knotted, and she tried to imagine how the conversation might have occurred between Kimmy and Doug. She shifted through the rack and pulled out a teal dress that she would have loved but the dress was too short and the neckline dipped too deep for her taste. She rejected a black dress that seemed too plain but spotted another one with a rounded neck, straight skirt with an embossed texture that added an interesting effect. She laid it over her arm and headed back to Kimmy's find.

The dress was indeed plum with a scoop neckline embellished with stones that glittered when the light hit them. A nice touch. The bodice and skirt were formfitting in a flattering way and the skirt looked as if it would touch her knees. The sleeves were short, but she already owned a black bolero-style jacket she could wear if the room was cool. In the same rack she spotted a similar black dress that looked more practical and she could wear a strand of pearls, but then did she want to be practical?

"Nina, here's one." Kimmy tugged at another dress in a hunter green, fuller in the skirt but with a longer sleeve and a bit of ruche in the bodice.

She saw Kimmy's excitement, and since it was a possibility, she selected that, too. "Okay, we have four dresses. I'll try them on. What do you say?"

"I say yes." Kimmy nestled close and followed her into a nearby dressing room. She settled on a bench and watched wide-eyed, as Nina tried on each dress, turning this way and that with Kimmy's oohs and aahs with each pose. After trying them all on, she tried to decide between the plain black and the plum color dress that Kimmy had spotted. She held up the two dresses. "Which do you like best?"

Kimmy stood and studied both dresses as if she were a high-fashion designer. "The black one is too plain."

This time she couldn't stifle her laugh. "That's what I thought. You have a good eye for dresses. You'll be a beauty when you grow up."

Her eyes widened. "I will?" Kimmy turned to look in the mirror and studied herself. "I guess I have to wait until I grow up."

"That'll come soon enough, sweetie."

She eyed the other three again, pressing her lips together and touching the material, then ran her finger over the sparkling stones. Nina managed to muzzle her chuckle. "I like the purple-colored one and not just 'cuz I picked it out. It's pretty and I like the color and Uncle Doug likes it, too. Buy the purple one."

Nina grinned, but she liked that one best, too, so Kimmy's opinion worked. She gathered the dresses, hung the three on the return rack and took Kimmy's hand as they headed back to the cashier. On the way, she spotted children's clothes, and as she drew closer, she saw a long-sleeved turquoise knit T-shirt with a rounded neckline and the word *cute* printed in block letters on the front. She grasped size seven and held it up to Kimmy. "Do you like this?"

"For you?" Her eyes sparkled.

"No, for you."

"I love it. It's so cute." Then she pointed to the block letters. "It says so right here."

"Then I think it's yours and you'll be cute in it."

"Uncle Doug will think you look beautiful in your new dress. I know he will."

Her mind snapped back to Kimmy's earlier admission. "Why do you know?"

Kimmy gave a big head shake. "'Cuz I asked him what color you would look pretty in."

"And he said purple?"

"First he said you looked pretty in everything."

Her eyes widened before she could stop them. "Really?"

Kimmy nodded again. "But then he said you would look pretty in purple because of your dark hair and lovely eyes." She hugged the T-shirt to her chest and turned away toward the checkout.

The words spiraled in Nina's head as she headed for the exit. Within minutes, she owned the dress, Kimmy had her gift and they were on their way back home. Though she enjoyed the time with Kimmy and buying the dress, she grew excited knowing she would see Doug soon. She couldn't wait until Saturday when he saw her dressed for a special occasion for the first time. She might even have her nails done.

The drive home took only minutes, and when she pulled in to Doug's, she slid out and turned toward the door, but as Kimmy ran ahead to the porch, she noticed she was carrying the shopping bag containing her dress. Then she recalled the package also held Kimmy's new top.

When Doug opened the door, Kimmy scurried in waving the bag. "Nina bought me a cute shirt." She giggled and dug into the bag until she came out with the purchase. "Look." She held it up.

Doug eyed Nina for a moment. "Did she ask you for—"

"Totally my idea. I thought it was darling."

Kimmy dropped the shirt into his hand, and he held it up again and fussed over it until she took it from him and ran to her room.

Nina gathered up the discarded sack and set it on a nearby chair. Before they could say a word, Kimmy trotted into the room.

"Nina, show Uncle Doug your new dress." She twirled to face Doug. "I helped find it and Nina loved it."

"You did?" He gave Nina a wink.

"Actually she did see it and showed me. I tried on four dresses and like this one the best."

Kimmy grasped the parcel. "Show him, Nina." She shoved it into Nina's hands.

"I'm ready for a viewing." Doug gave her a playful grin.

"You'll see it Saturday when I'm in it." She tilted her head waiting for Kimmy's challenge.

Doug gave a nod before looking at Kimmy. "I'm sure it will look better that way. Don't you, Kimmy?"

"Nina looks beautiful in it."

Doug gave Kimmy a smile and turned to Nina, his gaze capturing hers. "I'm sure she does. I'm looking forward to it." He tilted his head toward the sofa. "Won't you stay for a while?"

His expression drew her in, and mesmerized, she walked to the sofa and sank into the cushion. "Just for a few minutes. I'm sure you're hungry and ready for dinner. It's late."

"I planned on ordering a salad and pizza. How does that sound?"

Kimmy shouted a loud yes that sounded like a cheer. She skipped out of the room and Doug watched her for a moment. When she didn't return, he grinned. "Okay, now we can talk. Is pizza okay?"

Her stomach rumbled hearing him mention food. He gave an approving nod as if she had answered him. "Sounds great. Thanks."

"I'll call in a minute." He settled near her in his recliner. "I've been wanting to tell you something."

Her heart hit her throat, and she nearly choked. "Is something wrong?"

He gave her a vague grin. "Nothing like that." He drew in a breath and leaned forward, his hands folded on his knees. "When I mentioned that Angie suggested I be your escort for the wedding, I didn't lie but I twisted the facts a little."

"What do you mean you twisted the facts?" He looked uncomfortable, and though her curiosity screamed for an answer, she longed to soothe him.

"She mentioned the wedding and said she had a couple guests who couldn't make it and that she'd already finalized the head count, so would I like to attend." He paused, looking even more on edge, and studied her.

"And?" She could see there was more from his expression.

"I admitted that I would have loved being your date...escort. I knew you were going alone, and it seemed like a nice way to get to know..." He glanced again toward Kimmy's bedroom. "A nice way to get to know you better since we'd be alone."

"Alone at a wedding reception? I don't think so." She knew what he meant, but she needed to say something to break the tension.

He arched a brow. "Without seven-year-old ears listening."

She grinned. "I understand."

"So what I'm saying is after I said what I did, Angie jumped in and arranged the situation. Her comments gave me the courage to ask you. I'm sorry I didn't just admit it then, but—"

Seeing his discomfort, Nina rose and moved to the arm of his chair. "Doug." She looked into his eyes, her pulse thudding in her ears until it hindered her thoughts. "We are both careful with others. I know our reasons are different, and I don't know why you are as you are, but we are cautious when it comes to relationships. At least I sense that you are. You know I'm divorced. Getting involved, even dating, sends me a warning signal. I'm sorry I'm like that."

He shifted over to be on the couch and put his arm around her shoulder. "Do you mind? Are you comfortable?"

"This is nice." She had longed for him to be there, as senseless as it was.

Relief washed over his face. "I can't explain my problem exactly. It's a bundle of circumstances. I dated but never found anyone that I wanted to spend my life with. I wanted someone special. My sister got involved with that jerk, and their relationship was a disaster. And though my mom and dad had a comfortable relationship, it wasn't one full of fun and romance. I wanted more."

"Some marriages are like that, it seems."

"But is that the kind you want?" His eyes searched hers while his fingers brushed against her arm.

"My marriage became that kind, Doug. Sad but

true. No, I didn't want that, but I finally gave up trying and felt a failure." She pressed her hand on his. "So what happened to your parents?"

"My dad was diagnosed with diabetes in his midforties and didn't follow the doctor's orders. He ate poorly and played games with this medication. He ended up losing a foot and then his leg and then the other. Life was hard for my mother, and I devoted myself to helping them. After Roseanne learned she was expecting and the jerk split, I did all I could to help her." He shrugged. "I guess that's been my life, living other people's and not worrying about my own. But I never resented it."

"You wouldn't. That's the kind of man you are. I admire you for being like that."

"You do?" His eyes filled with questions.

"I admire a lot of things about you, Doug." A rush of warmth traveled up her arms where his fingers lay, and she longed to tell him what held her back, but the words wouldn't form in her mouth. Losing his friendship, the closeness that she enjoyed, could end if she revealed her huge shortcoming as a woman. Doug deserved children.

Doug drew her closer, his eyes searching, his arms protecting her, and as his lips neared, she longed for the kiss to happen, and today she knew it would. As his lips touched hers, Kimmy's voice severed the moment.

"Look at my top." She strutted across the living room posing like a runway model. When she neared, she faltered, and her eyes narrowed as if what she saw finally sank in. "Uncle Doug, you're hugging Nina."

Her awareness caused them both to react. Nina rose while Doug laughed and remained seated. "I noticed."

Kimmy missed the humor, but Nina had to work to hold back her laughter.

She moved to Kimmy's side and slipped her arm around her. "We were talking about serious things."

"Me?" Worry slipped to Kimmy's face.

"No, not you, sweetie. Uncle Doug was telling me why his father died. He would be your grandpa."

"I have a grandpa—Grandpa Bill."

"Grandpa Bill is my stepfather, honey. My birth father was in heaven before you were born." Doug beckoned her forward and slid her onto his lap. "He was sick and didn't take care himself even when Grandma told him he should, so he just got sicker and died."

"When I'm sick, I take medicine." She nestled against his chest.

"And look how healthy you are, plus you look really cute in your new top."

Concern flew from her face and changed to a smile. "That's 'cuz it says so right on the front."

Doug tousled her hair and slipped her feet to the floor. "If we're going to eat, I'd better make that call."

Kimmy skipped off again, and Nina relaxed, sensing Kimmy had forgotten what she had seen when she entered the room. But Nina couldn't forget her anticipation when Doug's lips touched hers. She could still taste the sweetness of his mouth on hers for that fleeting moment, and the one taste left her craving more.

Doug rang the doorbell. Since the near kiss, he could think of nothing else and anticipated seeing Nina in the new dress. He rarely wore a suit, not even for church, so tonight Nina would see him in his finery. He grinned at the silly thought.

The door opened, and his jaw dropped. Nina stood before him, striking in a plum-colored dress with glistening stones outlining the scooped neck. He stood outside mesmerized by what he saw. Her dark hair shone in the bit of sunlight still in the sky, and tonight she wore it loose and flowing around her shoulders. Her lips shimmered a shade of pink and her cheeks were bright with color. She had done something to her eyes, as if contoured in a dark color. Like a whirlpool, they drew him in.

"Are you okay?" She studied him as if confused.

"Tremendous. You look amazing." He released

a ragged breath and made it through the doorway. "The dress is gorgeous. I love the color."

"Kimmy said you liked purple."

Heat warmed his cheeks. "That girl talks too much." He grinned. "But she's right. I knew you'd be stunning in a color like this, and I love the sparkling stones." He leaned closer spotting her earrings that looked like diamonds.

"If you're wondering, they're faux diamonds. Definitely not real."

"But they're still effective." His chest constricted as a thought barreled into his mind. He could picture a real diamond on her finger, and the vision rippled along his spine.

She gave him a grin while her eyes searched his. "You look very handsome, but I knew you would. I love the tie, and did you realize it has a deep purple shade, almost plum like my dress? Did Kimmy tell you the color?"

"No. That's one thing she didn't tell me." He eyed her again from head to toe. "I realize you'd never seen me dressed up. I hoped you would approve."

"Doug, I more than approve. I'm proud to be dating you tonight."

She tilted her head as if questioning if he'd heard her. He had. "I'm honored to be dating you, too." He stood back, eyeing her from head to toe, flooded by the amazing outcome of events. "Are you ready?"

"I just need my coat. It's in the closet."

She drew it out, and he helped her slip it on. As they headed for the car, a feeling overwhelmed him. Tonight he was a man dating a beautiful woman, and a good one too with love for others, especially for Kimmy. She would make an amazing wife and mother. The thought broke through the lock he'd put on his emotions for the past month when he realized how he felt. Freedom wrapped around him, freedom to hope and dream for a brighter future.

And a real kiss.

Nina spotted familiar faces as the wedding guests made their way into the church. The church had an arrangement of three stained glass windows depicting Christ, the colors brilliantly lit by the autumn sun. The rich oak wood in the chancel glowed, the focus on a wooden cross, and the lovely baskets of flowers in shades of purple and white. She spotted calla lilies, chrysanthemums and lavender with touches of white carnations.

She and Doug chose aisle seats on the bride's side near the middle of the church. She looked around and spotted a few people she knew. El, accompanied by Birdie, sat a few rows in front of them. She still smiled seeing those two together. El had a forgiving heart along with his strong faith.

Doug pointed to his watch, and she grinned, seeing the wedding should have begun a few minutes earlier. Her creative mind at work, she thought of those horrible runaway bride or vanished groom stories and was happy to know that neither Angie nor Rick were the types to escape their wedding. Flinching, she imagined her own fears triggered those terrible ideas.

She eyed Doug, looking so handsome she lost her breath. When he arrived at the house, he'd looked at her with an expression she'd never seen before, not in his eyes or any man's before him. Todd had proposed and kissed her, but now that she'd met Doug, she acknowledged the truth. Todd's idea of romance paled in the light of what she had already seen reflected in Doug.

The music began as Rick and two attendants entered through a doorway at the front. Doug turned toward her, a gentle look on his face, and shifted his hand to hers. The warmth rolled up her arm and settled in her chest. When she had opened herself to possibilities, faint ones, her reaction to his looks, his scent, his touch sent her on an amazing emotional journey. A journey with apprehension but one she longed for.

The bridesmaids came down the aisle in lavender gowns. Their flowers were cascades in white and shades of violet. Nina thought of her plum-colored gown and smiled to herself.

Doug squeezed her hand as if he understood

her grin. He seemed to have an instinctive awareness of her. Sometimes that caused her to put
up her barricade. But today nothing about him
caused her concern, except the feeling she had
when she looked into his eyes.

A fanfare began, and she turned, knowing
Angie would be coming down the aisle. Instead
the children made their timid way forward,
coaxed by an adult as Carly sprinkled flower pet-
als on the white runner and the boy carried an
amethyst satin pillow.

Her emotions swelled as she heard the rustle of
excitement behind her. People rose, and when she
turned again to face the back, Angie had begun
her approach to the altar and to Rick. Nina wiped
tears from her eyes, remembering her own wedding wrapped in hope and expectations, all crumbled now and in a pile at her feet.

But today wasn't about her hurt. The day be-
longed to Angie and Rick, a couple she sensed
would have a long and happy life together. She
grinned at Angie as she passed, and Angie returned her smile, looking radiant. Her gown, embellished with tiny white flowers in the bodice,
fell into graceful folds to her feet.

When she faced the altar again, Rick's face
glowed with love and anticipation, and her heart
rejoiced at the beauty of this day. Doug slipped
his hand in hers again and when they were seated,
he rested his arm behind her on the pew. The

intimate coziness filled her emptiness, and she recognized the joy of having a partner to share the important things. She'd missed that so much in her life.

The vows began, and Doug leaned closer as he seemed to concentrate on the pastor's words, the same words that had captured her. "Do you promise to love her, comfort her, honor and keep her for better or worse, for richer or poorer, in sickness and health, and forsaking all others, be faithful only to her, for as long as you both shall live?" Rick's "I do" rang loud and sure, and the promise raced to her heart.

The words filled her mind and tangled in her heart. She knew Rick's abiding love would keep that promise, a promise Todd had uttered without thought. But a man of honor, a man who followed the Lord's commandments and His guidance would speak those words in truth. A man like Doug could do that. He could promise to keep a woman for better or worse, and he would mean it.

Shifting his arm from the pew back, Doug lowered it to her shoulders. His fingers brushed her arm and the warmth blanketed her with hope. *Lord, could this be?* She looked toward him, offering a reassuring grin. He drew her closer, and though an alert sounded in her mind, exhilaration overcame the warning.

The exchange of rings blurred in her head. So many images hung above her, all bringing pleasure and possibilities she'd longed for. A soloist sang, prayers were said, and soon Angie and Rick bounded down the aisle as man and wife. Nina's pulse skipped, watching joy radiate from Angie.

When the organ music rang out the end of the service, the wedding guests rose and filed toward the exit where Angie and Rick waited to greet them. As they inched along behind the others, Doug slipped his hand into hers, and she reveled in the comfort that spread through her.

Her eyes blurred with tears as they reached Angie and Rick. She gave them both a hug, and their warm welcome added to her growing assurance. Angie treated her like an old friend as she smiled and moved ahead with Doug to the parking lot to drive to the reception at the Comstock Inn.

Doug held the car door for her as she settled inside, and in moments, he joined her and slipped the key into the ignition but didn't turn it. Instead he turned toward her. "You were thinking about something during the wedding. Was it your own wedding years ago?"

He surprised her with his question, but the answer came with ease. "I did once, but only for a moment. I realized how sad it was and how I had misread so many things about Todd, I suppose in my eagerness to have a husband and begin my own life."

"I think that would be natural to have those

thoughts." He reached over and touched her hand. "I've never been married but I realized the seriousness along with the happiness. Marriage is a life change and a powerful commitment. I think Angie and Rick are headed for many years of good things."

She grinned, hearing him nearly echo her own thoughts. "That was part of what I was thinking about. With the right person, the vows spoken at a wedding can be a path for people to follow. Supporting one another in sickness and heath, for better or worse. Those words spoke to me. With a failed marriage in my past, considering another hasn't been on my list of possibilities, but the vow brightened my hope. I suppose reading the Bible and understanding how faith impacts a relationship is another important part of the *I dos*. Todd didn't have a speck of faith and mine had gone by the wayside. A divorce is built on empty promises and vows with no glue to make them stick."

"But you see things differently now. Is that what I hear you say?" Hope seemed to glow on his face.

"Yes. I need to digest it and its meaning for me, but I believe when a couple speaks those words in agreement, marriage has God's stamp of approval and His powerful support." Her admission wove into the fibers of her being.

Doug squeezed her arm and turned the key. He backed out of the space and rolled through the church parking lot toward the inn. She remained quiet, filled with ideas slipping into her mind and heart. Possibilities blossomed like flowers in Angie's bouquet, bright and fresh. With the new awareness, would her life change? Would bolted doors open? Or would she only be disappointed again?

Chapter Eight

Doug watched guests spill into the Comstock Inn Grand Ballroom and wished he and Nina could escape for a while until the food was served. He'd forgotten to eat lunch since his mind was filled with Nina and his expectation of the evening. He'd been forward during the wedding, holding her hand, and his heart sang when she didn't pull away. Her acceptance escalated his hopes for the evening. Yet sitting at the table with El and Birdie and others he knew put a damper on his plan.

Though he wasn't as new to the town, he'd never been inside the inn, but he was always impressed with the redbrick building with its white bay windows along the upper floors that stretched along Main Street. He particularly admired the colonial front porch with white pillars, and he watched Nina's expression as they pulled in.

"This looks like a lovely place for a reception, especially with Angie's color scheme."

Doug couldn't stop his grin. Men often missed those details thinking about the overall cost of a large wedding. Besides, he had a difficult time focusing on anything but her. Tonight Nina glowed, her hair color and eyes enriched by the deep hue of her dress.

He half listened to Nina chatting with El and Birdie, his mind focused on his hopes for the evening. With her openness to his romantic overtures, he rehashed how far he wanted to push, and he hoped he knew when to back off. He respected Nina and would never go beyond the bounds of what was moral and good, but since the day their lips touched in the fleeting kiss, he'd yearned to make it happen again but this time without interruption.

His gaze drifted to the miniature silver picture frame that listed their names and the table number that Nina said was a gift for guests. He loved seeing their names listed together as a couple, and yet he'd made a joke and asked her which half of the frame was his. So much for a romantic nuance.

"This room is a fantasy in white and various shades of purple." Nina ran her hand over the white linen with centerpieces filled with purple flowers and bound in wide white ribbons surrounded by small candles around the center display. "Don't you think this is gorgeous, Birdie? Look at the choice of flowers—lilies, dahlias and lavender blossoms—and I love the chairs covered in white and tied with the chiffon ribbon. It's glorious."

Birdie nodded. "It's very nice."

El gave him a wink, and they both grinned, but he couldn't resist his admission. "This reception could have bought them a mansion instead of living in Angie's house."

El and Birdie chuckled, but when he saw Nina's expression, he wished he'd kept the comment to himself. The cost hung in his mind but he let it fade, concerned that it would taint his enjoyment of the special day. Maybe his attitude would change if he ever…when he married. He liked hearing the more positive attitude for once. His mother would love it.

The mother idea struck his thoughts. Nina had mentioned Thanksgiving with her mother but nothing more was said. The open-ended topic left him curious. His wedding attendance was limited, and he'd forgotten how close people were seated. This was not a time for intimate conversation. It gave him even more motivation to find a place to talk.

El pointed to the other side of the room. "Anyone else ready to investigate the appetizers?"

Doug's stomach growled, and he looked toward the hors d'oeuvres. "I'm ready. Nina, what do you say?" She rose, and they made their way across the room. A wide selection of hot and cold dishes enticed him to try a little of many things and as they headed back, he stopped at the bar to pick up a club soda with lemon and an iced tea for Nina.

Before they reached their seats, the wedding party had arrived, and they hurried back to their seats, bypassing neighbors he barely knew. Though he was cordial, he preferred to enjoy the appetizers while watching the wedding reception tradition of introducing the wedding party.

With his disinterest in chitchat, time dragged. Nina tried to lure him into the conversation and he added a few words, but he wasn't one for small talk, except when he was alone with Nina, and then nothing was small talk. He listened to the dinner music performed by a string quartet and was relieved when the dinner service began.

Following the first course of salad and rolls, the highlight arrived, prime rib and chicken. With others focused on the food, he focused on Nina. "This meal reminds me of Thanksgiving. You mentioned your mother coming to visit. Is that still the plan?"

She didn't respond for a moment, then wiped her lips with the napkin. "It's not my plan but it's still on as far as I know. My plans have to be altered, I suppose."

Curious, he hoped she would go into detail, but instead, she sliced off a small piece of prime rib. "You're disappointed?"

She nodded. "I'd thought about inviting you

and Kimmy for dinner." She turned to him with disappointment in her eyes. "And if Roseanne is home, I would have been happy to include her, but now…"

"I would have enjoyed that." His chest weighted but no answer came. "Now it will be your mother and stepfather?"

"I suppose, and that not only frustrates me, but it makes me sad."

Her eyes searched his, but he felt at a loss to respond. But as the seconds ticked by, he asked the logical question. "Is there a reason you can't invite everyone? I'm happy to help with the meal, and—"

"Doug, it could end up being the worst Thanksgiving dinner of your life. My mom isn't easy to please, and it frustrates me. I don't want to spend the day defending myself in front of guests." She closed her eyes.

Sorry he'd chosen now to bring up the topic, he searched inside for a meaningful response. "I heard a tip once, and maybe you could try it. That is if you'd like to hear it."

Her eyes opened and she looked at him. "I'd like to hear anything that might work."

"No matter what she says, agree with her."

"Agree?" Her tone rose, and she caught herself and hushed.

"I know it sounds difficult but after you do it awhile it becomes easier."

Her brow wrinkled. "I'll think about that, Doug. It's an idea, if I can keep my mouth closed and do it." She gave him a grin. "My mouth doesn't like to be closed."

That made him chuckle. He loved knowing her traits so well.

Conversation rose around them as the meal ended, and he joined in as they discussed the good food. The dinner music had ended, the noise of the guests rose and a deejay was setting up in the same area. Soon, dancing would begin, and though it had been forever since he'd been on a dance floor, he suspected he could remember how. As so many said in that situation, it was like riding a bike.

Coffee and tea arrived, and soon the cake was cut and brought to the table. The dancing began with the traditional bride and groom dance followed by the wedding party, parents and all the folderol that went with a wedding. Nina's situation broke into his thoughts. What would she do for a wedding dance without parents she felt connected with? She had said she'd never marry again, but he sensed that would change, and he prayed he would be involved in that decision.

Having Kimmy in his care and Nina's positive approval had caused him to rethink his ability as a father. Maybe he would be a good one despite his lack of confidence.

The words encouraged him beyond his expectation. He wanted to be a father, and in the past months, he also wanted to be a husband.

"You're quiet."

He lifted his eyes to Nina's curious expression. "Sorry, I was thinking about weddings and..."

"The cost." She gave him an arched-brow look.

"No, not this time. I was thinking about the joy of it all." He gestured toward the dance floor. "Look at Angie and Rick. Happiness is written all over their faces."

She looked their way and smiled. "I've noticed. And they are very confident, which is so nice to see. And I think they'll have a great marriage... in sickness and in health. That's important."

The added addendum jarred him. He could see from her expression it had a meaning for her. Now he wondered if she had an illness and that's why she said marriage was impossible. Possibilities spiraled in his mind, but he only changed the subject. "And they're both so wonderful with Carly—they will make tremendous parents."

"Absolutely."

"I've talked to you about my doubt of being a good father. I don't like the feeling, but as I told you, I felt inadequate. But the other day at work, one of the men who just became a new father said something that made an impact on me. He said that no one is prepared for parenthood. It's learn as you go and different for everyone, but it's worth the effort and time. He put his hand on my shoulder and said that the reward of a child is far greater than the concern of whether or not I would be a good father." He held his breath watching her expression.

Her eyes lit. "He's a wise man, Doug. I've been telling you that you're wonderful with Kimmy, and if you'd made mistakes, you corrected them quickly. I've seen nothing but good things with you and Kimmy."

He slipped his hand over hers. "Thanks. I'm thinking I would like to be a father one day, even though I've said over and over I wouldn't."

"You need to be a father, Doug. You're one of the kindness, sweetest men I've ever met."

He loved hearing her say it, but her expression broke his heart. As the words left her, sadness slipped across her face. "Don't you want to have a child, Nina?"

"Yes, I do. Very much."

Her soft voice brushed past him, leaving him confused. Tony Bennett's voice filled the air, and instead of lingering in his thoughts, he drew her hand in his. "Would you like to dance? We can take advantage of this slow number."

Though she hesitated, she stood and followed him to the dance floor. When she stepped into his arms, warmth rushed through his body. Her thin frame lay in his arms and her sweet scent filled him with hope. The words of "The Way You Look Tonight" echoed his sentiments. Nina represented beauty without and within. Her heart opened to others and their needs. He'd seen that in his own life. And her love for Kimmy. How could she hesitate about having a child? It made no sense.

They moved in sync as if they'd danced together forever. Her breath brushed his cheek, and he longed to place his lips against her smooth skin. "You do look beautiful tonight, Nina."

Her head turned. "Thank you, and you're a handsome man, Doug."

The music ended, and she turned toward the table, but Etta James's voice filled the room, and she faltered. "Etta James. Do you mind? I love 'At Last.' It's such a meaningful song."

Mind? As the song said, he was in heaven. "Are you kidding? This is the best part of tonight."

She grinned. "Better than prime rib?"

"One hundred percent." He drew her closer this time, her head on his chest, her heart beating next to his. They glided across the floor, and when they were beside Angie and Rick, they smiled but he kept moving not wanting to break the rhythm of their movement or their hearts.

Exhilarated, his spirit soared as did his optimism. Despite her strange reaction to his question about having children, he hoped one day he would learn why. He'd learned too well that pushing Nina for answers caused her to raise a barricade between them. He couldn't take the chance.

Instead, he would be as patient as he could instead of barreling forward like an express train.

Etta James's voice faded away, and he spotted El and Birdie making their way across the room. He motioned toward them. "If they're leaving we should say goodbye."

She agreed, and he slipped his hand into hers and crossed the room. When they caught up with them, Doug laid his hand on El's shoulder. "Are you leaving?"

El chuckled. "Birdie and I fade away by ten so we're heading home. The food was good, and I even enjoyed some of the music."

Birdie nodded. "And we don't dance anymore." She gave El a sweet smile. "So nice to spend time with you both."

"Same here, Birdie." Nina gave her a hug, a sight he never expected to witness.

Before El said goodbye, he eased closer to Nina. "Drop by one of these days. I want to talk to you about something."

Her eyes widened, and while she grinned, her voice resounded with question. "I'd love to, El. I enjoy our conversations."

El gave her a nod and waved goodbye as he steered Birdie toward the exit.

Doug watched a second, and then slipped his hand back into Nina's. "We missed dessert. Look at that table full of sweets."

Nina patted her trim tummy. "I've had enough

food. I couldn't eat the cake. I'll probably wish I had some later."

Doug eyed the cake table and the pile of slices wrapped in napkins and ready to be taken home. "I can solve that problem when you're ready."

She chuckled when she saw where he pointed. "I know you have Kimmy on your mind and it's getting late. I'm ready if you are."

"Let's grab some cake to go...plus a piece for Kimmy, and when we get home, I'll make coffee or tea, decaf if you prefer, and we might be ready for the treat."

She smiled and gave an agreeable nod. They said good-night to Angie and Rick before leaving and hurried to the parking lot. The weather had grown colder, and Nina had only carried a light dress coat for warmth.

He needed nothing. Being with her warmed him body and soul.

Nina leaned her head against the passenger seat headrest, the words to Etta James's "At Last" filling her thoughts. Out of nowhere, Doug descended on her life. Her move to Lilac Circle had been for convenience and a new beginning. She lived closer to her work and away from the old memories. And while that was her plan, she learned that memories faded but the incidents that nailed them into her mind lingered like black mold, inciting a kind of deep illness that warped her view of life.

But little by little Doug and Kimmy had been the medicine that had healed Nina's wounds. Though memories remained as a scar, the rawness had faded. But tonight, without realizing, Doug had pried open the wound again with his question about having children.

Hope crumbled with the reality of her situation. Yes, she wanted children. She had longed for children, but she'd failed twice and after that her husband moved into another bedroom and was only a paycheck in her life until he left her. She could never go through that again, and tonight Doug had let her know that he wanted children. Not that he would like to have them, but he really wanted them. The words were similar but different. The want leveled her hope and the possibilities she'd allowed to fill her mind.

Before she roused and forced away her sadness, Doug pulled in front of Angie's house. "Wait here. I'll run in for Kimmy, and then we'll go to my place. I'm sure she's ready for bed by now."

Though going home would be better for her, Doug had suggested they eat the cake at his place, and she hadn't objected. That would have been the right time. She sat in the car with the heater warming her legs while he hurried in, and in moments he appeared on the porch with Kimmy in his arms. She slid out and opened the back passenger door, and he placed the half-sleeping child onto the seat.

The cold prickled down her spine and she slipped back inside as Doug rounded the car. When he opened the driver's door, another slap of cold sailed past her. When they pulled into his driveway, Kimmy stepped out, her eyes drowsy, and hurried behind him to get inside.

Nina followed, and once in the living room, she sat on the sofa, waiting for Doug to return from helping Kimmy get into bed. She weighed her options, either go home or stay, and when Doug returned wearing a grin, his expression made her decision. He chuckled. "She'd fallen asleep a short time ago. I hated to wake her, but—"

"She'll be sleeping again in a moment. Maybe already."

"Coffee, tea or…?"

"Either is fine, but make it decaf. I want to sleep tonight." She rose, but he waved her back to her seat.

"I'll bring it in here. It's more comfortable."

While she waited, her mind returned to her thoughts. The struggle continued between her heart and her head. Reason told her to pull back and let the relationship be a friendly neighbor. Her heart swung miles in the other direction. Let go and let God be in charge.

Unexpected tears blurred her eyes, and she closed them to stem the stream. She brushed the back of her hands beneath her lashes and opened them again. Though she'd been reading the Bible and knew the Bible said the Lord was almighty and with Him nothing was impossible, how could God fix her problem?

God could do anything. His words echoed in her mind, but her doubt remained. It would take a miracle like the parting of the Red Sea or the total darkening of the sun at noon to reverse her infertility.

The sound of mugs clinking reached her, and her pulse skipped. Should she be open and tell him? The answer fell on her heart. She wasn't ready to end their relationship. Maybe the Lord had something up His sleeve or why would He have brought them together to face more disappointment?

"It's decaf coffee. Is that okay?" Doug headed toward her with a wooden tray and set it on a small side table. "And cake."

His boyish excitement lifted her spirit. "What's a wedding without cake?"

"Agreed." He handed her the mug and set the cake on the lamp table beside her. Then he shifted to a nearby chair and sat. "What is this cake?" He ran his tongue over his lips after taking the first bite.

She thought a moment. "White chocolate with a hint of raspberry. That's what I taste."

He nodded. "That's it. I tasted the raspberry

but it was the white chocolate that threw me." He took another bite and gave her a wink.

The look rolled through her, and she watched him, unable to leave and yet unable to stay.

Finally he set down the plate and studied her a moment. "You said something at the wedding that made me curious."

Her memory ripped through the evening, fearing it was the statement she wanted to erase. She tried to look unconcerned while she held her breath. "I said a lot of things tonight."

"But this one made me wonder." He studied her serious expression.

It made no sense to delay the inevitable. "And what was that?"

"What you said about believing a great marriage happened when the couple believed in the vows, in sickness and in health." He shifted from his chair to the sofa and clasped her hand. "Nina, are you ill? Do you have cancer or MS or something that you think stops you from finding happiness in a marriage, because I don't think—"

"No, Doug. No. I don't have a terminal illness." Questions remained on his face. "I have nothing debilitating, nothing that will limit my life. I—"

"Nina, I'm so happy to hear that." He slipped his arm around her and drew her close, his eyes searching hers. "I could only think that you had a health issue so serious that you thought no one would love you. But that's not true, even if you were ill. Most people don't fall in love with good health or with perfect people. We… I fall in love with the person's heart and attributes. You are a beautiful person no matter what."

Tears pooled in her eyes, seeing his sincerity, and though she'd tried to avoid the truth, Doug loved her. Tonight dissolved any doubt she'd had.

Doug brushed his finger beneath her eyes, wiping away the dampness, tears she couldn't hide. His arms drew her closer, so close her heartbeat reverberated against his chest. His lips lowered as her breath depleted. His mouth covered hers, tender and sweet, then the feeling grew to a depth she'd never experienced, as if their hearts and souls melded as one. An amazing sense of wholeness washed over her.

He drew back, his gentle look kissing her eyes and filling her with joy. *Tell him. Tell him now.* The voice echoed in her mind as fear crept in and cocooned the admission she'd longed to release. Unwilling to ruin the amazing moment, the kiss she'd longed for, she let her confession lie for now, but soon—very soon—she had to tell him the truth of her fear.

Doug drew his hand along her hair, his eyes capturing hers, until he lowered his lips to hers again.

Silence filled the room as she rested her head on his shoulder and prayed for courage.

Chapter Nine

Doug studied the documents piled on his desk, weighing his clients' options to purchase new properties. He had two good choices to present, but as their advisor, he wanted to suggest options.

The word *option* settled in his mind. He'd decided to open up to Nina, and though he hadn't fully proclaimed his feelings, he sensed that she knew. The kiss validated his hope that she had similar feelings. The next step was to break though the blockade she'd put up to her past or whatever it was that made her veer away from commitment again. He'd prayed often and hoped the Lord—

His cell phone jarred him from his thoughts, and he pulled the phone from his desktop. Roseanne. His stomach hitched seeing her name. He couldn't help worrying. After two rings, he hit the talk button. "Hi, sis. Are you okay?"

"I'm great. I came home yesterday, and—"

"Why didn't you tell me? I could have come over and—"

"Doug, I have to know I can take care of myself. I knew you'd come, but then I wouldn't know how I'd do alone. But thanks for caring. You've already done more than anyone could ask."

"You're my sister. That's what family does." As the words left his mouth, Nina's family dangled in his mind.

"I'm ready for Kimmy to come home. I really miss her, and—"

"Are you sure, Roseanne? She'll add a lot of work to your life. Have you forgotten? I'm happy for her to stay until you're really up and stronger."

"Doug, I wouldn't ask for her back if I didn't think I could handle it. And she's seven. She can be a big help to me. I can't drive yet, but I can order food in and I have a connection with a grocery, which will deliver what I need. One of my neighbors will drop by and I'll have people come in to clean. Actually I often get help on that when my work becomes overwhelming."

"It sounds as if you've planned it well. Do you want to tell Kimmy yourself? She can call you when she gets home."

"Good idea. I'm sure she'll be thrilled."

He ended the call with her words ringing in his ears. Kimmy would be thrilled but he wouldn't. He'd miss her too much. Yet the experience had been validating and helped him know he was ready to be a dad to a little girl or boy. Even two or three children. He dropped the cell phone onto his desk and rubbed his temple. He had known the day would come, but he wasn't ready for it, especially so close to Christmas. And Nina would be disappointed without Kimmy there, he had no doubt.

The more he thought, the need to talk with Nina compelled him to call her now and not wait. He hit her phone number and listened to the ring.

"Hi, Doug. Aren't you at work?"

"I am, but I wanted to call you. Roseanne is home already."

"She is? That seems fast."

He heard concern in her voice. "I'm not sure she's ready to be alone, but I couldn't say much to her. She's determined she'll be fine, and then…" His voice caught in his throat.

"Then…what?" Silence except for the sound of open air. "Don't tell me she wants Kimmy home already."

"That's it. I'm… I don't know, Nina. I have no right to Kimmy but she's been so much a part of my life the past months I already feel lost—and even more important, I'd like Roseanne to wait and see how she does on her own first. Don't you think—"

"You're right. It's too rushed."

Her voice softened, and he recognized the same loss he'd experienced. His chest ached with the vision of being home in an empty house with no child's voice piping questions or needs. He loved being needed and being loved. He… "I'm almost speechless, Nina. I've never felt this way before."

"I've known Kimmy a much shorter time than you, Doug, and the loss still hurts. Sure, you'll see her over the holidays, but… It's not the same, is it?"

"No. I'll tell her tonight, and I'm sure she'll be happy, so I'll try to be happy, too."

"Doug, I'll be over when you get home or you can come here. Rema's visiting now, but we can talk more then, okay?"

"I have to go anyway. I have a pile of work in front of me and absolutely no desire to do anything…but the work goes on." He shook his head. "Thanks for understanding, and I'll see you later."

He ended the call, lowered the phone and placed it on the pile of documents and memos on his desk. Unable to concentrate, he caved against the chair back and drew in a breath, trying to digest his conversation with Roseanne. All he could do was tell Kimmy her mother wanted her back home, and then wait.

Waiting had become the bane of his life. He prayed one day the Lord would bless him with life moving forward.

When Nina returned to the living room, Rema watched from the sofa and scrutinized her with concern. "Is something wrong?"

She shrugged, hoping to cover her sadness. After she sank into the chair she had occupied earlier, she told her about Roseanne's hospital release.

Rema's expression relaxed. "Kimmy will be thrilled."

The comment pierced Nina's heart. "She will."

A frown returned to Rema's face. "But Doug isn't." Her frown deepened. "Neither are you."

"I am, I suppose. A child should be with her mom, but...from a selfish viewpoint, I'll miss her terribly. She's been a light in my life."

Rema's head tipped, her eyes searching Nina's face. "Doug's still here. Doesn't that help?"

A sense of guilt tore through her. Was it Kimmy who had captured her heart or...? She closed her eyes a moment trying to imagine life without him. "Doug makes it easier. We've become very good friends."

"Friends?" A faint grin curved Rema's lips.

"Good friends."

A laugh shot from Rema. "Are you trying to convince me or yourself?" She shook her head and rolled her eyes. "Nina, I would have to be blind to not see...even hear in your voice...how you really feel about Doug." She closed her eyes a moment. "Girl, you are in love."

Nina drew back, startled with the blunt comment. Did everyone interpret their relationship as love? She loved him, yes, but anything deeper than friendship…

"Frankly, I'm jealous, Nina. Trey's and my marriage was hopeless from the beginning, I fear."

"Why?"

"Because I saw things…suspected things, but refused to dig deeper. I closed my eyes and accepted his excuses for being late or having to travel for his work. After I looked back, once I realized he was having an affair—maybe more than one—I revisited those excuses. I should have used my brain, but…" She lowered her head and shook it. "I wanted to be married. All my friends had husbands and some with little ones, and I was envious. I felt as if I had the plague and couldn't get a husband."

Her heart weighted, hearing the truth of Rema's marriage. Situations like that were the kind she feared. How easy was it to be duped? How often did women or men allow their desire to marry hide the truth they were seeing but didn't want to admit? "I'm really sorry, Rema."

Her own failed marriage washed over her. She'd trusted him, never seeing the truth. Her husband was there for the better but not for the worse. "Sometimes, Rema, we want to trust so badly that we twist the facts to make them fit our want and not our need."

Need. What did she need? Her mind swam

in a sea of confused images. A good job. Hers was perfect. A cozy home. She had one. Faithful friends. She had new friends that she enjoyed. Someone to share her joys and sorrows? Someone to hold her when she cried? Someone to cuddle with at night?

If two lie down together, they will keep warm. But how can one keep warm alone?

The scripture floated through her mind on a wave of faith.

"You're right, Rema. I do love Doug, but sometimes I worry it's not in the plan. I've had one unsuccessful marriage, and I wonder if marriage again is meant to be."

"Why not?" Rema's eyes widened. "You were innocent. I tried to be a good wife. I did everything I could to make Trey happy. You didn't know me when I didn't do a thing. No classes, no friends, no job. He wanted me home. I hated my life, but I did it for him. Then I realized why he wanted that. If I stayed home, I wouldn't hear the rumors of his carousing."

A lump formed in Nina's throat, imagining a life controlled by another. Being under someone's thumb with no movement. No activities. No joy. Nothing. "God gave you a blessing, Rema. Yes, in a strange way, going against His Own Word, in a way. But I believe the Lord plans our steps despite the course we devised."

Her response knocked her cold. Chills rolled up her arms and down her back. Had she determined that she would never fall in love again and now the Lord was showing her otherwise?

"I'm not a big churchgoer, Nina, but I do have faith, and yes, I agree. Look at me now. I'm a person. An individual who is enjoying life. I take yoga and I've met a very nice man. He's not pushy. He's friendly and kind. He's invited me to stop for coffee after the class. I'm not looking for anything now. It's too soon, but it lets me know that maybe I'm a little bit appealing."

"Little bit? Rema, you're very pretty."

Rema grinned. "I fixed myself up a little. Got a nice haircut, bought cosmetics and learned how to use them." She chuckled. "That was another class I took. Can you believe? I found a night school class that teaches improving self-image."

Nina rose and gave Rema a hug. "You look lovely, and I'm glad you took the class. If we don't love ourselves, it's difficult for others to love us." She shook her head. "Except maybe our parents, and then that's not a guarantee."

Rema hugged her back. "You've become a good friend, Nina. Thank you. It's so nice to visit people and not think I'm like a termite appearing at their door and wanting to be friends. I always felt people were kind but standoffish. That's not a good feeling."

She nodded, unable to imagine having self-esteem that devastating.

"Now at least I can smile." She grinned. "But I need to go. I have dinner planned with a couple of women I met at the self-image class. It's fun to hear what's happening in their lives. I never wanted to be a glamorous model. I just didn't want to feel like a termite."

Nina shifted back while Rema's frank admission lifted her spirits. "You amaze me, Rema. I can't even picture you in that way. It makes me realize we can create an image of ourselves, and then work to change it for the better."

"Positively." Rema pushed herself up from the sofa. "Thanks for the great talk, and I hope everything turns out for the best with Kimmy. I know it will be difficult when she's gone. Children can fill a life with love and noise. Both can be missed." She chuckled.

Nina walked her to the door, and after saying goodbye, she stood a moment digesting everything that had been said and what it meant. She'd heard herself say things that had new meaning the longer she thought about them.

She wandered to the kitchen, pulled out a diet pop and eased into a chair. What did the Lord have planned for her? Was He guiding her away from the images she had created for her life and changing her steps to His plan? A plan that included Doug?

A new weight struck her heart. Doug deserved children and she couldn't give him those with her issues. But with God all things were possible. Could it be? She loved Kimmy. Could she have a child one day? Lowering her head, tears spilled from her eyes and rolled down her cheeks, a few dripping to the table.

Changes. What needed to be done? Like an arrow, Thanksgiving shot into her thoughts. Maybe having company could soften her mother's negativity? No, not her mother. Shame rose like a dragon. She backed away from her thought. Anything could happen. She wasn't in charge. Things could change.

Her mental argument gave way to a solution. She would host Thanksgiving dinner for Doug, Roseanne, Kimmy and her parents, God willing.

God willing times two. She needed assurance.

Doug observed the smile on Kimmy's face with a heavy heart. When her mother told her the news, he'd managed a contrived smile that must have resembled a grimace forced upward at the edges.

After her bubbling excitement, her expression faded. "But I won't be here for Christmas and the decorations. Nina said we could make acorns with ribbons and sparkles."

Despite his ache, a smile eased the tension in his face. "I think you mean pinecones."

She tittered and gave him a toothy grin. "One with the little ruffles all around."

A novel way to explain it. He was smiling now, inside and out. "That's right. The one with ruffles. But don't worry about that. Nina will make sure you get to make decorations with pinecones."

Her concern fell away, and she turned to look behind her. "Where's Nina?"

"She's home, but she said she'd come down to visit."

A deep frown inched to her face. "Is she mad at me?"

"Mad? Why in the world would she be mad?"

Her eyes lowered to the carpet. "'Cuz I'm not going to be here for Christmas."

"Am I mad?" He managed another grin and hoped it looked sincere.

"No, but... I'll miss you and Nina every day. I have fun living with you, Uncle Doug. You do things with me and take me to the park, and..."

Her lip trembled, and he opened his arms and drew her in. "Kimmy, you can come here whenever your mom agrees. We're not that far away that I can't pick you up at school and bring you here." His arms tightened around her for himself as much as for her. "We can still have fun and do things."

She brushed the tears from her eyes with the

back of her hand. "Momma needs me to help her, but… Uncle Doug…"

His lungs constricted. "What, Kimmy? Are you worried?"

"I don't know how to do things, and maybe she needs me to—"

"Sweetheart, she doesn't want you to cook dinner and clean the house. Your mom just wants you there. She misses you." The words hit the air as they hit his heart. Roseanne did need her reassurance. She'd faced a life-and-death situation, and his hope was that she'd learned what was precious in her life. It wasn't giving her life to her work. Kimmy was her most precious gift, and he could only pray she realized it now.

Kimmy lifted her gaze, the concern gliding from her face. "I can be there. Are you sure that's all?"

"I'm sure." His prayer rose that Roseanne hadn't forgotten that Kimmy was only seven. "I want to take you someplace special before you go back home, so I'll check with your mom. How's that?"

"Where?"

Her eyes lit up brighter than he'd seen them since the conversation had begun. "It's a surprise."

"But—"

"No buts. You'll find out soon enough."

"Can Nina go, too?" She searched his face.

"Would I go to a fun place without Nina?"

Her head swung back and forth in a flurry. "It's more fun with Nina."

A chuckle rose from his throat. "I agree. She's terrific."

"And you like her a lot, don't you. A real lot."

His pulse skipped. If Kimmy read his feelings, who else realized how much he cared? Heat burned in his chest and climbed upward. "I do like her a lot…a real lot."

"I know. I think you love her, Uncle Doug. Do you think so?"

She'd cornered him. The longer he remained quiet the more she probed with her eyes. "I think I do, Kimmy. What do you think about that?"

"I think…yippee. I love her, too."

He released a deep breath as he watched her expressive face. Kids came up with too many truths at times. Honesty was on the tip of their tongues and sometimes it needed to be. He knew how he felt, but saying it made it real. Real and amazing.

A soft knock punctuated the moment, and he hurried to the door with Kimmy on his heels.

When he opened the door, Kimmy threw herself into Nina's arms. "Uncle Doug wants to take us to a surprise." She studied Nina's face as she tried to get inside with Kimmy clinging to her. "Do you know the surprise?"

Nina's questioning eyes captured his. "I don't. So it's a surprise for both of us." She grasped

Kimmy's hand and they closed the distance. "What is it?"

"It's a surprise." He motioned for her to sit. "But not today. We'll go tomorrow in the late morning. It's supposed to be pleasant weather, but I have to make sure that's okay with Roseanne."

Her expression told him she understood. She wandered across the room and sank onto the sofa. "Do you want to hear my surprise?"

Kimmy plopped beside her. "You have a surprise, too?" Her intent gaze clung to Nina's.

Nina tousled her hair. "It won't be after I tell you." She lifted her eyes to his. "I've decided to have everyone for Thanksgiving if that works for Roseanne."

"My mom?" Kimmy's eyes widened. "Is my mom coming to your house for Thanksgiving?"

"I hope so, and you'll meet my mom then, too."

"Yours?" Her eyes widened more.

Nina grinned. "I have a mom and a dad, Kimmy, just like you." Her mouth snapped closed as if she realized Kimmy had no father, only a father she'd never known and one she thought had died.

She held her breath, waiting for Kimmy to ask a question or make a comment.

"I hope Mommy can come to Thanksgiving 'cuz otherwise we'll be home alone."

Doug's tense shoulders lowered, relieved she'd let the reference to a father pass without a thought. "We'll work out something, sweetheart. Don't worry."

She thought a moment, and then bounded from the sofa to his side. "Call Mom, and see if I can stay here until after the surprise."

He drew her into his arms and gave her a squeeze. "I'm sure she'll agree but I'll call so you don't worry." He sent her to sit with Nina, knowing he'd have to explain and went into the kitchen to call his sister, praying she would agree.

When he returned, he tried to keep his expression serious. "I talked with your mom."

Kimmy leaped from the sofa into his arms. "What did she say?"

"She said…yes!"

Kimmy shot from his arms, piping her happiness as she twirled around the room and dive-bombed onto the sofa beside Nina.

He and Nina roared while Kimmy sent them a smile that warmed his heart.

Chapter Ten

On Saturday afternoon, as Doug drove away from town, Nina watched the signs as they passed and wasn't surprised when they approached a large barn with a Country Corn Maze placard on the side. Cars dotted the parking lot, as it was late in the season, but the weather had allowed the maze to remain open until the first frost would end the fun-filled event.

Kimmy began to squirm behind her, her shoes kicking against the seat back as she leaned in every direction, trying to figure out where they were going. "This is a barn. Are we seeing animals?"

"Read the sign, Kimmy." Nina pointed to the red-and-white sign in the peak of the red barn.

She squinted through the side window. "What's a corn maze?"

Doug flashed her a grin. "Wait and see."

When the car stopped, Kimmy flung open the

door and slipped out, but Nina wasn't far behind. "Kimmy, don't forget to watch for cars. This is a parking lot and cars might pull into this space. You know what could happen?"

She looked at the open door and frowned. "The car could hit Uncle Doug's car."

"Worse than that, it could hit you."

Her eyes widened. "I'll be careful next time."

Nina gave her a pat. "Good. I won't worry then."

Kimmy studied the huge corn patch. "What do we do here?"

"Have you ever worked on a puzzle?"

Kimmy nodded with questions in her eyes.

"A maze is sort of like that. You start down a path and try to find your way out the other end."

Kimmy's eyes lit up. "I have puzzles like that in a book. I try to draw a line to the end but I keep running into paths that stop."

"That's it. Same idea." As they followed Doug, she slipped her arm around Kimmy's shoulders, too aware that these special moments would soon end.

"Do they find us if we get lost?"

The concern in Kimmy's voice made Nina grin. "No, they give you clues along the way so we can get back. Anyway, your uncle Doug wouldn't let us get lost."

She agreed and skipped on ahead to slip in next to Doug. Nina stood back and watched the two, anticipating the loss they would feel when Kimmy was gone. Though he'd planned the special day for them, the corn maze couldn't stop the ache in her heart.

As she neared, she couldn't believe her eyes. "Angie, I had no idea you guys would be here."

Angie tilted her head toward Rick. "He wanted to come earlier but things got in the way so today he announced do or die we were coming to the corn maze. His excuse was Carly had never been to one. But the truth is Rick's more excited than we are."

Nina chuckled, suspecting Doug edged out Kimmy and her, too. "This will be great for the girls."

"Carly whined on the way here about not having a friend along. She'll be happy now."

When Doug and Rick approached them with a map, they had already turned the maze into a contest with the loser paying for dinner.

She shook her head and grinned, forgetting how competitive men were at times. Angie caught on and gave her an "I understand" look. The group headed off to the entrance, and after deciding which path to follow, Rick darted ahead with Angie running along beside him. Carly begged Doug to let Kimmy be on their team, and he finally agreed, hurrying ahead to make sure the girls caught up.

Nina ambled along, assuming Doug would

wait for her. When she turned the next bend and realized she had choices, she stopped and looked around, trying to guess which way they had gone.

Before she panicked, Doug returned, a grin plastered on his face. "I thought you'd followed me."

She raised her shoulders and let them drop. "No, I thought this was a fun outing and not a race to the finish."

From his expression, he got her point and slipped his hand into hers. "I've got you."

His warm hand pressed hers, and the heat rose up her arm and to her heart. After a few false turns and no sign of Rick and the others, they found one of the checkpoints. Doug picked up the paper punch and made a hole in the map.

"What's that for?"

"It's another contest. If you find all the checkpoints on your part of the maze, you turn it in. Later they'll do a draw for the large pumpkin." He chuckled. "You've always wanted one of those, haven't you?"

The expression on his face made her laugh, a feeling she'd learned to cherish. Thoughts of her past soared through her. Days that passed without laughter. There had been some pleasant days, but after the miscarriages. the darker days had overshadowed the bright ones.

Doug squeezed her hand again and heat rushed to her heart. When he stopped and looked at her, she lifted her free hand to touch her cheek for a flush, but it was cool. "Why are you looking at me like that?"

"Because you're beautiful."

Her breathing became shallow. "I'm what?" She shook her head. "If you said *beautiful*, you need to have your—"

He moved in front of her and captured her cheeks between his hands. "I have perfect vision. No need to have them checked. We see differently. I see a woman with a generous heart and a loving spirit. A woman with brown, glowing eyes and dark hair with highlights of sunshine." He brushed his hand along her hairline to the nape of her neck.

Chills ran down her back, but his eyes wrapped her in a kindled glow.

"Nina, I've been single all my life without any regrets until now."

A frown tugged at her face. "Why now? Because you've enjoyed Kimmy and now you want to have—"

"Because I've met you, and I feel whole for the first time in my life."

"Whole? I—I don't understand."

"You live alone, Nina, but once you lived with someone…when you were married. Doesn't life seem different now than it did when you had someone in your life?"

She had someone in her life. Doug…and

Kimmy until she moved back home with her mother. "I had to adjust, but sometimes alone is better than together in misery."

"But I'm not in misery anymore. In the past year, I felt lonely at times, but mostly I didn't realize what I was missing. Now I do. I don't like the feeling of coming home from work to no one."

She drew in a breath, her chest tightening with an awareness she didn't recognize. Doug's expression, the way his eyes searched hers, the closeness of his face left her weak and longing for him to hold her close.

"Nina, I'll miss Kimmy. There's no doubt about that, but what I would miss even more is you if you walked away. Sometimes I fear that's what you will do."

Reality washed over her. "I'm not going anywhere, Doug. I enjoy your company too much. I care about you."

He lowered his hands to her shoulders and drew her closer. His tenderness spread through her, and when his lips lowered, she raised hers to meet him. All fears, all concerns sailed away on the breeze and the rustle of dried cornstalks became the music of her heart. His kiss deepened, and she yielded to feelings she had blocked. Today they soared, caught in the rush of longing and hope that had escaped her for too long.

Voices rippled over the dried stalks, and Kimmy's giggle crackled in her ears. Doug eased back and looked toward the sound. "I think we have visitors." He slipped his hand into hers as the girls darted around the corner.

"Where have you been?" Kimmy's fist rested on her waist but this time she looked concerned. "We waited for you."

Nina gathered her wits and managed a guilt-ridden smile she hoped Kimmy didn't recognize. "Maybe we were waiting for you."

Kimmy shook her head. "You got lost, didn't you?"

Lost in each other's arms, but that wasn't the answer she could give Kimmy. "No, we're just being slow."

"You're supposed to be fast and win the race." She flagged them forward.

Doug gave her an "I surrender" look.

Nina trotted off behind the girls, not caring who bought who dinner. She'd opened her heart and with that came a cavern of worries she would resolve. Doug needed to know the truth before he met her mother, who had never spent time with her without reminding her that she couldn't have children.

Doug deserved more than getting smacked that way. She'd opened her heart to him when they were alone, and now she had to not only open her heart but also her past.

The truth would set her free one way or another. She prayed it wasn't the other—being alone again without Doug.

But she had to take a chance.

Doug stood in Kimmy's bedroom, once again a guest room, and watched her pack the last of her belongings. He'd helped her assemble a boxful of toys and books she'd collected during her stay. His gaze swept the room, which looked empty already, exactly as he felt.

His reaction to Kimmy's return home was not only about his feelings. He was also concerned about the situation Kimmy was going home to. Roseanne seemed to think she was well enough to handle the bundle of energy he'd lived with— and loved—the past months. He had more than second thoughts.

Kimmy's move had drawn his mind from Nina and the amazing kiss in the corn maze. He longed to know where she stood with her feelings. If the kiss was the barometer, she cared as much as he did, but sometimes his instinct failed. Today he teetered with that concern.

Instinct about Kimmy's return home flailed in the same way. His emotions tangled with his own desire. Maybe he wasn't thinking about what was best for her and Roseanne.

"I think I have all my clothes, Uncle Doug." Kimmy scrutinized her luggage and turned to face him. Though excitement had bounced around her the night before, today when she began packing her eyes had a moist glow.

He strolled next to her as if to check the contents of her bag, but instead, he slipped his arm around her shoulders and gave her a hug. Her reaction startled him. "I don't feel good."

"What's wrong, sweetie?"

"My head hurts and my tummy is sick." She swung around and buried her face in his hip, tears flowing.

Doug crouched down and cuddled her in his arms, his own heart torn by her response to the hug. "Kimmy, you'll feel better when you get home. Making changes is hard for us, but I know you want to be with your mom, and I'm still going to see you a lot. And so is Nina."

"I want to help my mom, but I want to be here, too." She choked on the comment and sobs broke free.

Doug wasn't sure if she felt guilty balancing her two emotions or if it was the leaving itself that really made her so sad.

"Kimmy, I'll miss you, too. I've loved having you here, and if your mom decides you'd be better staying here a little longer, she'll let you come back. But I know she's so anxious to have you home. You're an angel, Kimmy, and I know you'll love being home once you've been there a couple of days."

She pulled her head up and nodded, but her expression revealed her struggle.

"Where's Nina? I thought she was going with us."

"She's on her way over."

He closed her suitcase, gave a last look at the room and slipped his arm around Kimmy's shoulders. "If you forget something, I'll bring it over for you. Okay?"

"Okay."

The doorbell rang, and Kimmy broke free of his arm and rushed to the door. When she saw Nina, she reached up and gave her a hug, and again tears rimmed her eyes.

Nina knelt beside her and talked so softly he couldn't make out the words. Kimmy clung to what she said as if her words were gold. When her tears faded, he carried the luggage out to the car.

In moments, Kimmy and Nina came from the house, deep in conversation, but this time, Kimmy had a faint smile on her lips. Doug grasped the image and prayed it would get him through the final steps of the trek to Roseanne's.

While Doug made coffee, Nina sat in the living room reliving the difficult goodbyes. Though Kimmy had whispered she was sick, her reaction when she saw her mother eased the pain of saying goodbye. Though Kimmy longed to be in two places at once, her mother's presence added a surety to her move back home.

She had clung to them during the goodbyes, but Doug promised to visit often and she guaranteed she'd make the Christmas pinecone ornaments with Kimmy. Those promises eased the difficult parting. But outside, tears had blurred her vision, too. She turned back to the doorway, where Kimmy watched them climb into the car. Nina had waved and blew a kiss and Kimmy returned it and eased the door closed. As they pulled away, she spotted Doug brushing away the emotion from his eyes. And now she sat in his living room, anticipating the silence.

Doug returned with two mugs of coffee, and she grasped one, warming her icy hands, too aware of where the conversation had to lead.

The corn maze had been her undoing. Doug's gentle touch, the vulnerable look in his eyes, the nearness of his lips to hers had broken the barrier of her full emotions. Love poured out in the kiss they'd shared, and she'd revealed herself to him. It was too late to put on the brakes. She'd driven full speed ahead, and now she had to face either walking away or telling the truth. At Thanksgiving dinner, she knew her mother would reveal the truth if Nina hadn't already. But how should she begin?

She took a sip of the hot coffee and fell into

silence, her thoughts writhing with all she had to say.

"This is silly."

Doug's voice jarred her thoughts as tension thrashed through her. Did he suspect she had something to say? "What's silly?"

He gave her a hopeless look. "I'm a grown man and can't believe I'm acting like this." He ran his finger beneath his moist eyes.

"It's not silly, Doug. That little girl got under my skin, too, and I'm not calling it silly. I'm calling it love."

He eyed her as if surprised at her response, and yet he must have known how she felt.

"One day you'll have your own kids, Nina. Think how hard it must be to say goodbye when they strike out on their own."

His response smacked her chest and drained the air from her lungs. He'd opened the door to her admission, and now her mouth twitched with the jumbled words she needed to say. "I'm sure saying goodbye in any circumstance is difficult." The feeble response was all she could think of in the moment. She needed to organize her thoughts.

"As much as I worry about Roseanne hobbling around, I suppose I need to give her credit."

Her stomach knotted when he returned the subject back to Roseanne.

"I don't want to see her depending too much on Kimmy for things. I hope—"

"Doug, I understand your concern, but as we both agreed on our way home, you have to wait and see. Don't you think Roseanne will admit if it's not working? If she needs too much help, she'll realize Kimmy's a handful. Getting her back and forth to school will be the biggest issue."

"She said another parent agreed to pick up Kimmy when she took her daughter to school. I hope that works as planned."

"You can pray that it works. Did you forget?"

He chuckled, and it was the first time that day he'd shown any lightheartedness.

Tension faded from his face, and her pulse raced, knowing she had to dampen his spirit again with the truth she had to reveal. She swallowed bile that rose to her throat and sent up a prayer.

"Doug..."

He studied her, a scowl revisiting his smooth brow, and his reaction wrenched her confidence.

"You said something a second ago that...that I need to talk with you about."

"What? What did I say? If I hurt your feelings or—"

"No. It's nothing like that. It's what I haven't said that's the problem, Doug. Something I don't tell anyone, but I must explain it to you because it's important."

His scowl deepened and he shifted closer and

sank into a chair. "What's wrong, Nina? I can tell it's serious, and I—"

"Yes, it is serious because it's something I know is important to you. A few seconds ago, you said one day I would have children of my own, but…but that isn't going to happen, Doug."

His jaw dropped and his mouth opened as he took a deep breath. "What do you mean?"

Pressure weighted her chest and knotted her vocal cords. She waited a moment to get control before she could bring her voice to life. "My marriage ended because of the situation."

"What situation, Nina. Just tell me." A desperate look filled his face and broke her heart.

"I had two miscarriages, Doug, and the doctor found a problem that will cause me never to carry a child to full term."

His face twisted from desperation to confusion. Silence hung between them, and nausea rose upward, plowing into the back of her throat. She fought back the sensation, praying one of her rare prayers for God's guidance. "I wanted children badly. As much as any woman who loves children, but it didn't happen. Do I blame God or do I blame something I've done or—"

"Nina, please. Blame no one. Life hands out joys and sorrows."

He quieted as if in thought and she feared talking, asking, knowing what had muted his voice. She had offered him a piece of news no man wanted to hear, not one who deserved to be a father and would be a good one.

After time passed, her love for him nudged her to offer an out to his dilemma. "Doug, I understand your confusion. Yes, I care about you with all my heart. I tried to lock my feelings inside and let you know that I was serious about never marrying, but I failed miserably. My actions were unfair to you. I loved your kisses and the corn maze undid me."

"I'd been undone before that, Nina. You're not to blame, and somehow I believe that the Lord moved us to these feelings. He opened my eyes to what I had been missing. You showed me what companionship is like. You opened my eyes to feelings I'd locked away. You're not alone with that ability to conceal things through avoidance. I'd dedicated my life to family and watched marriages falter and crumble. They held no interest for me."

She searched his face, seeing his heart shine in his eyes.

"And then came Kimmy. I adored her always. She's been the cutest child, creative and a bundle of charm. Spending time with her for these past weeks made me realize what marriage can be. It doesn't have to be a failure filled with problems. Love can heal everything, and I knew I would never marry unless I saw my marriage filled to the brim with love."

"But now a relationship with me is different. I cannot give you or any man the children that you long for. A marriage to me can't grow into a family. It's a couple, a childless couple. But you don't have to live with that, Doug."

Tears broke from her eyes and blurred her vision. Seeing him in a haze relieved her from seeing the disappointment in his face, the sadness in his eyes. "I'm sorry. I'm so sorry that I let it go too long without warning you."

Doug lifted his head, a new expression on his face. "No blame and no sorrys, Nina. First, it's not your fault. It's life. Many couples are childless and many by choice. Second, do you believe the words of one doctor? Did you have a second opinion? Will you explain what's wrong that you assume you can't carry a child through the nine months?"

The intimacy of her problem knotted in her throat, but she owed him details. "It's a chronic disease that can eventually result in more serious illnesses. It's hard to treat. After my first loss, I went on the medication. We were so sure but it happened again. The doctor believed that medication wasn't the answer. Even with surgery, having a child is far from guaranteed. Any treatment is close to hopeless."

He shook his head as if he could dislodge the problem from her body. "Nothing is hopeless. Second opinions, new medical treatments...in the medical field new discoveries are made daily."

Any response she could make seemed empty. She'd once had hope but it had left her three years earlier when Todd walked out and ended their marriage.

"But, Nina, if that's the problem that's holding you back from loving me I can live without my own children. Kimmy's my niece and I love her as deeply as I would a child of my own. Why would I feel any different with an adopted child? Love given has nothing to do with blood running through the veins. It has to do with what's in your heart."

His words touched her to the depth of her being, but her own needs struck her. "I would want to give my husband a child. A little person that's a blend of the husband and wife. I want—"

"Do you care what I want, Nina? Do my wants and hopes mean nothing to you? I'm being honest with you. Yes, I would love a child of my own, and you would, too, but what happens if I can't have children? That's a possibility. I would only have some guarantee with tests. Would you expect me to have them—or any man—before accepting his proposal?"

Her throat ached from holding back sobs. "No. Never, Doug. I wouldn't think of such a thing."

"Neither would I. So here's my request. Would you please visit another doctor for a second opinion or for new treatments? Don't accept never, Nina."

She looked away, and then raised her head. "After Thanksgiving. I'll give it thought."

"Nina, the outcome wouldn't change my feelings about you, not one iota, but you might have hope again, and I want that for you."

Tears broke free, and Doug drew her to his chest, holding her against his heart. She opened the floodgate and let the salty water flow down her cheeks and onto his sweater.

He swayed as a father might for his crying child, and she clung to him, wrapped in his care and concern. He'd never flinched at her confession. He'd been thoughtful but steady in his gaze. For once, she knew she could trust him fully. He meant what he said.

Now it was in her hands.

Chapter Eleven

Nina slipped on her jacket, grasped the container of cookies and headed down the street toward El's. Each time she read something in the Bible, her talk with El came to mind as did Doug's request for her to visit a new physician. This time she didn't need the cookies as an excuse, but he loved them and who didn't enjoy an appreciative fan?

When she pushed his bell, the door flew open, and she faced a young woman she'd never seen before. "Is El in? I'm a neighbor." She motioned toward her house and waited while the stranger gawked at her a moment before she turned and headed back inside, leaving the door open. "Gramps. Another of your lady friends is here."

Nina grinned, certain Birdie had hustled over seeing a woman she didn't know visit El.

El's chuckle reached her ears as he came through the archway. "Nina. I'm so glad you came." He pushed open the storm door and she entered. As she did, he eyed the container and his grin grew broader. "And you came bearing gifts."

"I hope you like them."

He accepted the container and gave her a playful look. "If they're sweet, you know I'll love them." He motioned for her to sit as he continued past her. "Ginger, can you come here a minute?"

"What?" She ambled in, a scowl growing on her face. "I'm busy."

He eyed her a moment, and Nina sensed he had sent up a prayer. "I hope you can spare a minute. I'd like you to meet one of my neighbors."

Ginger shrugged and looked at Nina. "Hi." She turned away.

Before she could leave, El touched her arm. "Ginger, this is Nina. She lives in the house at the corner."

"Okay."

Nina forced a pleasant look. "It's nice to meet you, Ginger. How long are you visiting?"

Her eyes shifted to El and back as if she were uncertain.

"Ginger will be staying here for a while." He arched an eyebrow and looked at her.

Ginger squirmed under El's gaze. "Right. It's here or jail."

Her blunt response threw Nina off balance. An appropriate response swirled through her head.

"I'm sorry, Ginger, but you have a wonderful grandfather, so the choice was a good one."

Ginger pressed her lips together though a faint grin sneaked to the edge of her lips. "I suppose you're right." She turned to El. "Is this necessary, Gramps?"

He opened the container and offered her a cookie.

Ginger eyed the treats a moment, and then took one. "I don't mean to be rude, but I know if I didn't tell you, Gramps would."

Another challenge. She sought a response and decided honesty was best. "Sometimes getting things out in the open is better than skirting the issue or lying. I've skirted the truth often, Ginger, and I want to tell you it's caused me more grief than I can explain."

Somehow what she said caught Ginger's attention. This time she gave up the battle and let her grin come through. "You sound like my grandpa. He says things like that."

"That's because it's true. I've spent my life hiding something about myself that'd kept me from moving forward and being happy."

Ginger backed up and dropped into an easy chair. "Really?"

"Really. In fact, that's part of the reason I dropped by today, hoping I'd catch El alone so I could talk with him about it."

"What's the other reason?" Ginger narrowed her eyes.

"The last time I saw him, he asked me to come over because he had something to talk about."

El chuckled and settled into his recliner. "I don't need to say much now, Nina. You've just opened the door to why I wanted to see you. I watched you and Doug together at Angie's wedding, and I recognized two people who were in love, and yet I could still see a kind of hesitation in your behavior. Something unsettled you. Only a faint hint of it, but I've seen it too often. It's like the day I gave you Margie's Bible."

"You gave her Grandma's Bible? Why?" Ginger's voice had an edge.

Nina's head jerked. "Ginger, if you'd like your grandmother's Bible, I'd be happy to give it to you. I've read so much of it and—"

"No." Ginger shook her head. "I was just surprised. Gramps always kept that Bible beside his bed. It was as if he kept a little of Grandma with him."

"That's true, Ginger." Nostalgia filled El's face. "But I've begun to heal, and I thought your grandma would like someone to read it who really needed to learn about Jesus."

"You weren't a Christian?" Ginger's jaw sagged.

"A very watery one at one time, but the water had dried up and so had I."

Ginger nodded as if she understood. "Gramps

is right. I have a Bible. I just don't read it anymore. I fell for a guy with a dark past. I let him drag me down with him." She shook her head. "I hate talking about it."

Nina understood and resisted questions. Ginger would talk more when she was ready, just as she'd learned to do.

"Are you ready for this, El?"

"Sure am, but only if you're ready to talk with an old geezer like me."

"El, I've told you many times. A wise old geezer like you. You're filled with more wisdom than anyone I know."

He grinned, while she gritted her teeth, wanting to hold back the story she'd come to tell, and yet she could see it served even more purpose with Ginger there. She eased her back against the sofa cushion and drew in a breath. She started from the beginning and spilled the details into the space between them, one that had been silent except for her voice. "And then I met Doug, a man who God meant to be a tremendous father and a good husband. But, El, I am caught with my situation."

"You have a situation, but are you really caught in it?"

"Not as much as I was. I finally confessed what held me back from falling in love and being a wife."

"Doug didn't walk out on you, did he?" El tilted his head as he waited for her response.

"You know he didn't. But he asked me questions and made me think."

El leaned closer. "Questions?"

An ache grew in her chest. "He wanted to know how many doctors I'd talked with. I said one." She shook her head. "So he asked me to have a second opinion."

"And that's frightening, isn't it?"

She nodded, her gaze sweeping across Ginger's face, filled with her own pain.

Forcing her gaze from Ginger, she sorted through her thoughts. "Yes, but it made me act. I went online and researched. I learned some things that helped me to understand Doug's question. Medical advances happen daily, and doctors do make mistakes. My problem is very similar to another female issue, and that one has a new surgical procedure that helps, but…"

El's gaze grew tender. "But what if you get your hopes up, and your first doctor was correct."

She nodded, a ragged breath tearing from her lungs.

"But, Nina…" Ginger's voice shot past her. "What if your first doctor was wrong? What if you can have a child? What if you turn down love that would be wonderful just because of a what-if?"

"Smart girl, Ginger." Pride rose in El's voice.

"Those are good questions. And here's another thought. My Margie had some kind of female problem, and the doctor warned her that it was a good possibility she would never have a child."

"Really, Gramps?"

He gave Ginger a nod, and then shifted his gaze back to Nina. "She kept that a secret for a short time, but I sensed something was wrong. I didn't bug her. Margie wasn't one you wanted to bug."

Ginger chuckled. "Grandma liked life to run her way."

El gave Ginger a watch-what-you-say look. "One day, Margie told me, and I said I loved her for her and I reminded her the Lord was in charge. He would decide." He chuckled. "I was right. Within a year, Margie was expecting our first daughter, and a couple years later we had our second." He smacked his knees and rose. "See what I mean. We're not in charge."

"So I should trust that Doug is telling me the truth. He will still love me if I go through with another doctor and learn the same thing. No babies."

El's expression answered the question.

"That's what I thought, but I wanted validation, El. I value your opinion. Very much."

Ginger scooted to the edge of her seat. "So you'll get the second opinion?"

Nina nodded. "I've looked up a few doctors,

and I'll call for an appointment as soon as I get past Thanksgiving."

El crossed to her side. "That's the best thing to do, Nina, and I'll pray the answer blesses you, no matter what it is."

"Me, too." Ginger nodded.

Ginger's offer startled her. "Thank you." Nina rose and took a step toward the door. "Ginger, I'm happy to listen anytime, and, El, thank you so much."

He opened his arms, and she stepped in and accepted his hug. Outside she had a bounce to her step she hadn't had earlier. Her decision was made and El had validated it. The truth was what she needed. She would learn to live with it.

Nina opened the oven and basted the turkey, golden brown, the way she liked it. She eyed the wall clock, and her pulse skipped. Her mother and stepfather would arrive soon. She looked heavenward for the nth time and asked the Lord to help her deal with her mother's criticisms.

The potatoes boiled in the large kettle and she turned down the burner. She'd prepared well. The vegetable casserole was already baked and ready to slip into the microwave for a warm-up, and she'd done the same with her corn casserole, one of her favorites. She grinned, picturing Doug, who'd insisted he would take care of dessert.

Her cell phone's ringtone began, and she crossed to the table and grasped it. "Doug. Are you—"

"We're just leaving. Kimmy's still not feeling well, but Roseanne is pretty good. I guess it's a trade-off."

"Poor Kimmy. I thought once she'd adjusted to home she'd be okay."

"Me, too. I think she needs to see a doctor, but Roseanne can't take her so I'll suggest Roseanne make an appointment for next week. If she needs a ride, I'll take her."

"Good idea. My mother isn't here yet but I expect her anytime now. I'll see you soon." Their call ended and she returned to the last-minute details to burn off her anxiety.

As she closed the oven, a horn reverberated from the driveway. She hurried to the front, managing a pleasant expression. When she opened the door her mother had reached the porch with her stepfather on her heels. "Mother, you made it. How was the trip?"

"As good as can be expected." She stood a moment scanning the front of the house.

Nina nodded to Howard and waited to hear her mother's evaluation.

"I thought it would be bigger." Her mother arched a brow and grabbed the doorjamb as she made her way inside.

"It's big enough for me, Mom. One person doesn't use a lot of space."

"One person doesn't. Too bad. I think women should have a husband, but then I guess you have other ideas."

She squelched her rebuttal and avoided agreeing with her. The agree-with-her technique was meant to be used at selected times. It was the best way to stop an argument. "Have a seat. Dinner's in the oven. Would you like some coffee or tea?"

"What brand of coffee?"

Nina ignored her mother's expression. "I have a coffeemaker with individual cups. Would you like to see what I have?"

"Never mind. Give me something bold." She flashed a look at Howard. "He'll drink anything."

Howard's lengthy sigh whispered in the air. "Anything."

She returned to the kitchen, grateful for the break to regroup and pray for her patience. With the two coffee mugs in hand, she joined them and sank into a chair across from them. "How have you been?"

Her mother shrugged. "Nothing earthshaking. The question is how are you?"

"Good. Very good. In fact, I have some friends joining us for dinner. I hope you don't mind."

Her mother's eyes widened. "Friends? Why would you—"

"Because it's Thanksgiving, Mom, and I'm

thankful for the friendship I have with Doug and his family."

"Doug?" She flashed a look at Howard again. "Who's this Doug?"

"A neighbor. I met him shortly after I moved here. They had an end-of-summer block party, and—"

"Block party? Goodness." She snorted. "This is a small town. I've never seen a block party in—"

"Big cities don't always have them, I suppose, but it was a wonderful way for me to meet my neighbors. I'm not a coffee klatch type person, but I know if I need help where I can go."

"Why do you need help, Nina? You've always been very independent. You don't listen to anyone's advice. For example, when you lost that first baby—"

Patience flew out the window and no technique could stop her. "Mother, that was four years ago. Do we have to relive that again?"

"I only meant—"

"I know what you meant." Nina forced her fists open. "You enjoy reminding me of—"

Noise at the door saved her from herself.

"They're here." She held up a finger and hurried across the room. "Come in. You're right on time." She gave Doug a look she hoped he understood.

He gave her a wink and shifted for Kimmy's

entrance, but instead of her bounding inside, she walked in, a look on her face that caused Nina to be concerned. She bent over and pressed her cheek to the child's. "Are you feeling any better?"

Kimmy shook her head, and then noticed the company. Her eyes shifted to Nina's.

"This is my mother and stepfather, Kimmy." She eyed them again and gave a timid wave.

She'd never seen Kimmy that shy and her concern rose. She looked at Doug, holding the door open for Roseanne, and he only lifted a brow.

Roseanne swung in on crutches and Doug followed. With the three inside the door, she motioned toward her family. "Mother. Howard. These are my friends, Doug, his sister, Roseanne, who you can see is recuperating from leg injuries, and Roseanne's daughter, Kimmy."

She turned to them. "This is my mother, Alice, and my stepfather, Howard."

They exchanged greetings, though her mother and Howard sat without making an effort to stand to welcome them.

Doug faltered to a stop. "I forgot to bring in the dessert." He held up his index finger and retreated through the doorway.

Roseanne settled in an easy chair with an ottoman while Kimmy sat beside her on the floor. Before she could offer drinks, Doug returned carrying two pies and something in a paper bag.

She took drink orders and followed Doug into the kitchen.

As soon as he set the pies on the counter, he turned and drew her into his arms. "You don't look happy."

She released a long breath. "It's tedious already, but I'm doing okay. Hopefully with you here, she will soften up a bit."

"I'm sorry, Nina. You don't need any added stress in your life." He drew her closer, his lips lowering to her mouth.

Since she'd explained her inability to have children, each kiss became more precious, a validation that he hadn't abandoned her. His request entered her mind and her thoughtful talk with El. Ginger, of all people, had said something that touched her. What if the doctor was wrong? She'd convinced herself that never was reality. Never left out God's hand on her life.

"What can I do to help?"

Doug's voice drew her back and made her smile. His willingness to do anything came naturally to him, and she loved it. "How are you at carving turkeys?"

"A pro." He chuckled.

"I'll take that answer with a grain of salt...or even a grain of sage, but you'll do a better job than I will."

She opened the oven and he brought out the golden-brown bird and set it on a cutting board while she slipped the corn casserole inside to warm it. After she popped the veggie casserole into the microwave, she hurried back into the living room, hearing her mother ask questions about Roseanne's accident and the whereabouts of Roseanne's husband. She winced, seeing Roseanne's uneasiness as she said they had separated years earlier.

Grateful that her mother didn't ask more, she was even more grateful she'd interrupted the conversation. "We're finishing up in the kitchen. The food will be on the table in a few minutes."

"Can I help?" Kimmy rose from the floor and crossed to her.

"If you want to. Can you carry things to the table?"

Kimmy nodded, too quiet in comparison to her usual enthusiasm.

She set out the cranberry relish she'd made and a tray of relishes for Kimmy to carry into the dining room while she slipped the dinner rolls into the oven. The corn casserole had warmed, and the microwave beeped as the veggies were finished.

Doug filled a platter with turkey and she grabbed a masher and attacked the drained potatoes. Soon the food was ready and she invited everyone to the dining room table. Once everyone had gathered around, she shifted her attention to Kimmy. "Would you like to say the blessing?"

Kimmy nodded, and from her peripheral vision, she noted the shocked look on her mother's face. Everyone folded their hands except her mother and Howard as Kimmy began the prayer. "Come, Lord Jesus, be our guest and let these gifts to us be blessed. Amen."

Again Roseanne, Doug and she reiterated the amen though her mother and Howard continued to remain silent.

"This dining room is a bit small, wouldn't you say?"

Time for her technique. "Yes, it is for a large group, but we seem to fit just fine."

Her mother looked away and sliced a sliver from her turkey.

Though Roseanne had been quiet, she accidentally helped Nina's plight with her mother. "The turkey's excellent, Nina. It's moist and such a good flavor. Do you do something special?"

The questioned brightened Nina's day. "Nothing but baste it often."

"Well, it's delicious."

She grinned at Roseanne. "Thanks, but maybe it's Doug's carving."

Doug smiled at her and dug into the corn casserole. "Now, this is excellent."

Nina's spirits rose. Despite her mother's scrutinizing, hearing compliments relaxed her. She knew her mother wouldn't try her negativity on the company.

Kimmy only picked at her food, so unlike her, and Nina's concern deepened as she watched. When she asked to be excused, she beckoned to Kimmy to come to her and felt her cheeks and forehead. Heat penetrated her hand.

Roseanne noticed. "Does she have a fever?"

"I think so." Nina pulled her hands way. "I can take her temperature."

"I'm guessing it's the flu." Roseanne shrugged and, with a grimace, shifted her leg, obviously still in pain.

With the meal concluded—and enjoyed from everyone's comments—Nina suggested saving dessert for later. Doug and her mother rose and began to put away the food, so she sneaked off for a moment with Kimmy to take her temperature.

When she read the results, her concern turned to worry. The thermometer read a hundred and three degrees. She found Doug in the kitchen, and after she told him he said he would warn Roseanne.

Nina struggled to concentrate on the conversation, distracted by Kimmy's health. Her mother's acerbic comments lessened, and she fell into conversation with Doug about his work and Roseanne's situation. Nina was even more surprised to hear her mother talk about her father's illness and death. Since her mother said little about those days, hearing her speak in a positive light about her dad touched Nina's heart.

She placed her hand on Kimmy's forehead to check the heat again, and this time her mother noticed. "Nina, you seem to be preoccupied with Kimmy. It's such a shame you don't have children of your own."

Though the comment might have slipped by the others as a remark from a caring mother, Nina saw it as another way to belittle her. The dig bit into her self-esteem once again and dampened her spirit.

Doug leaned back and gave her an understanding look before addressing her mother. "You know some women enjoy waiting to have a family until the time is right. Who knows what the future holds for Nina? I know she could make an amazing mother. She has lots of love to give to a child. Ask Kimmy."

Kimmy nestled closer to her, lifting a faint smile.

Her mother's comment dropped to the floor while Kimmy's reaction sent her to the sky.

Nina watched her mother's eyes shift from Doug to Kimmy to her, and she said nothing. Doug had come to her aid and she loved him for that. Loved him for many things.

Despite being store-bought, the dessert was a hit—a pumpkin and a French silk pie. Each took a slice of their favorite and Doug tried both. He'd brought along a can of real whipped cream, and the pie and coffee finished off a successful meal.

Though Roseanne's focus turned to Kimmy, she began to look achy. Doug noticed the situation and rose. "I think I need to get this patient back home, and we can take a good look at this young lady." He scooped Kimmy into his arms, and despite her illness, she giggled. The sound delighted Nina, and even her mother made a kind comment.

After the others slipped out the door, Doug leaned in and squeezed her hand. "I'll see you later. I want to get them home, and I'm as worried as you are about Kimmy. I don't think this is the flu."

"I agree. I think Roseanne is beginning to realize Kimmy's sicker than she suspected."

From his expression, she knew he wanted to kiss her goodbye, but with her parents watching from the sofa, he winked and hurried to unlock the car.

When she closed the door, her mother gave her a questioning look. "Are you not telling me something?"

"Like what?" She kept her voice casual, not willing to open her heart.

"You know 'like what,' Nina." A frown edged her face and grew. "This man is more than a nice neighbor. You two have a connection. I watched you through the day with your little looks, and you love that girl, don't you?"

"Yes, Mom, I do. She's sweet and fun. Kimmy's a creative, wonderful child."

"But it's not his child, right?" Her frown eased to curiosity.

She nodded. "Right. She's his sister's but she's been alone for years raising Kimmy and Doug is always there for her. He'll make an amazing father."

Tension eased from her mother's face. "He would make a good husband, too. I hope you see that."

She gave an evasive nod.

"Does he know about your problem?" The lift of her voice communicated her assumption.

But Nina had a response ready. "Yes, he does."

"Really?" Her pitch arched somewhere between surprise and question. "And he understands."

"Doug cares about me for me, Mom. And though I believe he will handle it if I can't carry a child, he suggested I get a second opinion. Medical advances have been made since the last diagnosis."

Her mother lowered her head and shook it, leaving Nina to wonder what it meant.

"I appreciate his gallantry, but I'm not sure the reality has hit him yet. I don't want you to get your hopes up, Nina. The doctor seemed confident when he gave you the verdict. What if you go through more doctors and tests, and the first doctor was correct?"

Though her comment sounded negative, Nina witnessed true caring in her mother's eyes. She opened her mouth to respond but Howard's voice slipped in first and startled her.

"Alice, what happens if the doctor was wrong, and Nina could have a child? Isn't it worth the chance?"

At this moment, Nina loved her stepfather. "That's how I see it, too, Howard. I've avoided thinking about it, but I care greatly for Doug, and yes, Mom, I can see him as a wonderful husband. One who would stand by me no matter what. I want to give him a chance to have children with me."

"I agree. If you are willing to take the chance on being disappointed, then I support your decision. I would be a good grandmother, Nina, although I doubt if you agree."

"Mom, I don't know what I think. You and I have butted heads for a long time, and—"

"You were Daddy's little girl. I was your mother, and I suppose I was jealous."

Her eyes widened before she could digest what her mother had said. "I had no idea you felt that way, Mom. Lots of girls are Daddy's little—"

"I suppose their mothers are confident that they are good parents. I didn't have much of a role model, but I did the best I could. I know I failed in many ways. I wanted you to be perfect so people would know I raised a lovely daughter, but you couldn't hide your disdain for me, Nina. The more I sensed your feelings, the more I tried to build myself up by—"

"Finding faults with me." Her chest ached, controlling her emotion. "Mom, I didn't know. I never suspected. I thought you didn't like me or that I was a horrible disappointment. You talked about only my flaws, all negatives. I never knew you saw anything positive."

"My defense. I'm sorry about that. Howard noticed and finally said something and I analyzed my behavior. He was right."

"But when you arrived you…"

"I slipped into my old self. You know it's hard to break bad habits, Nina. But now that I have explained, I hope you can understand even if you can't forgive me."

She released a stream of air. "I can forgive you. Forgive you with all my heart." She opened her arms and her mother rose and hugged her for the first time in years.

"But let me bug you again. If you are thinking about this, what do you plan to do?"

"I'm going to find out all I can about my problem. I've already done some research and investigated a doctor. But this time I'll go with ammunition and this time maybe I can find an answer."

Her mother smiled. "And I'll keep my fingers crossed."

"Thank you, Mom. That means the world to me."

Doug plowed through paperwork in his office, grateful today he didn't have clients to see since he was distracted, waiting to hear about Kimmy.

After he'd taken Roseanne home and started to leave, she had asked him to stay for a while so he could help with Kimmy while she tried to make arrangements to see a doctor the next day. Roseanne dealt with an answering service, and a while later the doctor finally called. Doug watched her struggle through the conversation. Though Roseanne was grateful that the physician had returned her call, she appeared to struggle to keep an even tone while she begged him to see Kimmy the next day rather than take her to emergency.

Doug agreed. The wait would be forever on Thanksgiving Day and Kimmy had become nauseated and could keep nothing down. Waiting in an emergency room was no place for a sick child.

He offered to drive Roseanne to the appointment, but she called in the morning to say a friend had agreed to drive them to the doctor's office. And now he waited, his heart in his throat.

His distraction wasn't only Kimmy. Nina had

been on his mind when Kimmy wasn't. He'd made a quick call to her the past evening to tell her where he was. He longed to talk with her about the Thanksgiving dinner experience, but there wasn't time. He'd left Roseanne's late and he'd been in a rush this morning. He'd wait to call until he had news. When his cell phone rang, he grabbed it, his pulse pummeling before he realized the caller was Nina.

"I thought you were Roseanne."

"You're upset. What happened last night?"

He filled her in as quickly as he could. "I'm now waiting for Roseanne to call. I don't know what's happening at this point."

"Please let me know and I'll be praying it's nothing serious."

He'd prayed, too, but he continued to worry. "I'll call you when I hear something."

After he disconnected, his mind shifted to Nina and her mother. He could understand why their relationship had been strained, and no matter what solution he considered, the situation had a hopeless feeling. Yet he knew better. Something could make a change, but he had yet to think of anything.

Forcing his mind back to his work, he managed to complete a plan of action for one of his clients, and outlined some financial steps for another who wanted to expand his business and his real estate.

When his ringtone jarred him again, he knew

it was Roseanne. He hit the talk button and listened, his apprehension growing. "What does that mean? Isn't meningitis serious?"

"There's two kinds, according to the doctor, and the tests will tell us which."

Two kinds. Questions filled his mind but Roseanne's distress caused him to hold the questions for later. "What can I do to help?"

A sigh breathed across the phone. "I can't ask my friend to spend much more time here. She's taking us to the hospital for the tests, but she can't wait. I'll need a ride home, hopefully with Kimmy."

She choked and he recognized the beginning of her tears. "I'll get there as fast as I can. Where will you be?"

"Probably in the medical building for the blood work and X-rays, but maybe not since you'll be a while before getting here."

"I'm not waiting, Roseanne. I'll talk to my boss, and I'm sure he'll give me the rest of the day off. I'm not that far." They hung up and Doug hurried into his boss's office. His work could wait. He needed to be by Kimmy's side.

Nina sat in her home office and checked her watch again. She'd thought Doug would call earlier. Time had ticked by and she'd heard nothing. While waiting, she decided to do more research on the diagnosis that explained her inability to carry a child. Doug could be right. New treatments and information were found daily. She'd hoped that something could make a difference, but she'd found nothing specific that gave her hope.

When she clicked on another link, she came to the section on diagnosis. She scanned the options and spotted the test she'd had—laparoscopy. She read the article and words jumped out at her. The test was only 60 percent accurate. The doctor had never told her that.

Knowing internet facts could be wrong, she found another article, one from a reputable hospital, and she was certain the information would be accurate. Her heart skipped as she read. Only 45 to 67 percent of suspected lesions were confirmed as accurate. Twenty percent found that the positive finding in laparoscopy would be incorrect.

Her heart soared. Hope she'd given up on for years could be renewed. Maybe, just maybe, she was one of that 20 percent.

Overwhelmed by her findings, she rose from the computer and wandered into the kitchen. It was too early to eat, but her stomach had rebelled since she'd begun her wait. She searched the fridge and found a couple of apples in the fruit drawer. She withdrew the smaller one, cut it into pieces and headed to the living room. As soon as she popped a piece of apple in her mouth, her cell phone rang. She dug into her pants pocket.

"I got off work early to give Roseanne a hand. She'll need a ride home. They're at the hospital for some tests. The doctor thinks Kimmy has meningitis."

The diagnosis wrenched air from her lungs, and all thoughts of her research faded from her mind, filled by Kimmy's diagnosis. "That's serious, isn't it?"

"Roseanne said there are two kinds. The tests are supposed to determine which."

"Doug, is it okay if I go, too? I can't sit here. Can I meet you there?"

"Please, Nina. I know you love Kimmy. I'm not sure where she'll be and I don't know what will happen after the tests, but you can ask where she is at the information desk. That's what I'll have to do."

"See you soon. I'm on my way." She hit End and pulled her coat from the closet. Nothing could keep her from being there with Doug. Racked with concern, she headed for the door, then gathered her wits and returned to grab her purse before she darted to the car.

She drove to the end of Lilac Circle, turned right and then left onto Hickory Street and right onto King Street. Her heart hammered as she followed the highway and once she crossed Shiawassee, she knew she was almost there.

After parking, she made her way inside, located the first information desk and received directions to the waiting room where she hoped to see Doug. To her relief, he was there.

When she stepped into the room, he rose and she rushed into his arms, anxiety writhing through her body. "Have you heard anything?"

"Roseanne is with her. We're still waiting to hear the test results. They did blood work and X-rays. And Roseanne said they might do another test. It was PCR or something like that."

"What's that for?"

He shrugged. "Roseanne said the doctor suspects viral meningitis which is less serious, so they're checking for viruses to determine the best treatment. If it's not viral, it might be bacterial, and she'll need a spinal tap. That's more serious."

"No, Doug. Please, Lord, let it be viral only." She lowered her head, her mind spinning.

"I'm a knot of nerves, too. But I really feel for Roseanne. She's so scared and blaming herself."

Her head drew back. "Why? That doesn't make sense. If anybody's to blame, it's you and me. We've been with her for months." The possibility devastated her. "But what did we do wrong?"

"Nina, no one's to blame. People get sick. Bacteria is everywhere and viruses fill the air. We can't fix that. Let's wait and see what the tests show."

He backed toward his chair and patted the one next to him. "Sit with me, and we'll wait. We can't do much else. I can go down to the room or you could, and see what Roseanne knows, but I think she would have told us if she knew anything more." She nodded, too anxious to think of anything better to do. She sank into the chair and leaned back her head as she drew in a breath.

"I ran out of the house so fast, I almost left my purse."

He chuckled and snapped his fingers. "We need a distraction. Tell me what happened after I left on Thanksgiving. How did it go with your mother?"

"Amazing. I was anxious to tell you, and then with all this I forgot." She related the change in her mother—and in herself. "I think it was a step forward, Doug. It's not perfect, I suppose, but we made strides. Now I understand partly what happened, but I can't picture my mother jealous of my dad. She always came across as confident in her actions. As if she were always right and the rest of the world was wrong."

"People sometimes do the opposite of what their real feelings dictate. It's a cover-up. If they can't fool themselves about their feelings, they can fool other people by their behavior. Have you ever seen a guilty person?"

She grinned. "Yes, and they do everything to hide their guilt. You're right."

"I'm guessing that's what your mother did. It would have been hard for her to admit she was jealous of her own husband."

"You're right." The idea worked through her mind, and she took one more step forward. "I need to find ways to develop a relationship with her. It's been at a standstill for so long."

"You'll think of something." His grin tingled down her spine. She sank into silence, her mind sorting through the past and clearing the cobwebs of confusion that she'd faced for too many years.

Doug slipped his hand into hers and gave it a squeeze. Feeling his nearness and his overpowering effect on her, she sank into a kind of peace. Learning there was a possibility her diagnosis could be wrong would stay buried for now. Kimmy's health was all-important, and she needed to learn more before she could be confident in the hope she'd felt. She would read more, and then act.

"Mr. Billings."

Doug jumped, hearing his name. He rose and headed to the desk. In a moment, he turned back to her. "Roseanne said I can come to the room. The doctor is there."

He paused a moment and she knew what bothered him. "Doug, you go. I'll wait here and pray it's good news."

He gave her a questioning look until she rose and gave him a quick kiss. "I prefer to wait. You're family. I'm not." But oh how she wished she were.

He gave her another look before turning toward the door and hurrying out.

She folded her hands, her gaze clinging to the empty doorway. Though prayer was still new for her, she'd been surprised how easily it came with each prayer. She bowed her head and prayed the Lord's blessing on Kimmy. That's all that mattered.

Chapter Twelve

Doug stood in the doorway, his chest aching. Kimmy looked so tiny, covered in hospital sheets and a blanket. She appeared to have drifted to sleep, and Roseanne's eyes were closed in prayer or she'd also fallen victim to exhaustion.

He crept into the room, but Roseanne's eyes flew open with a startled expression. "Sorry. I fell asleep, I guess. I'm as worn-out as an old rug."

"You should be, sis." He drew to her side and gave her a hug. "What did you hear from the doctor?"

She gazed at him as if part of her had remained in dreamland. Finally the glaze left. "He's still waiting on the last test, but he is quite certain she has viral meningitis, which, believe it or not, is good news."

"You mentioned it was less serious. Praise the Lord if he's right."

She nodded. "I'm torn, Doug. They want to

keep her overnight to administer an antibiotic and keep her fever down until they're certain that it's a virus. They told me to leave and they would call if there's a problem, but I don't think I can. I don't want her to wake and be afraid when I'm not here."

"I know it's difficult to leave, but you need your rest. And you don't want to spend time in the hospital. If your immune system is compromised from the surgery and recovery, you could easily catch something here. It happens."

She gave him a grave look. "I know, and here's the worse news. Viral meningitis can be contagious. They'll know more when they get the test results back. Sometimes it's not."

"So that gives you greater reason to get home and rest. Would you feel better leaving after you talk with Kimmy? She is a smart girl and she will probably understand and give you permission to go home without being upset. Why don't you decide after you talk with her?"

She studied him a moment without responding. After drawing in a lengthy breath, she looked into his eyes. "I know you're right. Let me talk to her and I'll make a wiser decision then."

He could only nod in agreement to her idea. He looked into his own heart and realized how difficult it would be to go home and leave a little one in the hospital. "Nina's in the waiting room. I know she'd like to see Kimmy. Would you mind?"

"Not at all, bring her down. Maybe Kimmy will wake up soon and we can all see her."

He gave her shoulder a squeeze and slipped into the hallway, praying that his advice would come true. Kimmy wasn't a whiner or a child who needed reassurance. She had gumption for her age, and he sensed she would want her mother to go home. His thought became a prayer as he returned to the waiting room.

As soon as he stepped in, Nina's eyes met his and he beckoned her to follow him. She rose and met him outside the doorway. "How is she?"

"Sleeping, but I'm sure she'll wake up soon. They want Kimmy to stay overnight until they're sure about a few things." He gave her the details. "I'd like Roseanne to go home for the night so I'm hoping when she talks to Kimmy, she'll agree."

"I'm sure it would be hard to leave, but for her own health, that would be best."

He slipped his arm around her back as they finished the trek to Kimmy's room. When they stepped inside, he noticed Kimmy had turned on her side and seemed to be waking.

Her eyes widened. "Uncle Doug. Nina." She studied them a moment. "I had tests and now I have to stay overnight." She glanced at Roseanne. "I've never been in a hospital but they are nice. I like the nurses 'cuz they talk to me and make me laugh." She giggled. "And they brought me ice cream in a little cup."

He grinned. "Ice cream in a cup makes the hospital not such a bad place, doesn't it?"

She tittered again. "Mom?" Her grin faded. "But you can't stay here 'cuz there's only one bed." She patted the mattress. "And this one isn't big enough for you and me."

Roseanne gave him a glance before she responded. "No, I would have to sit in a chair."

Kimmy shook her head. "You can't sleep in a chair, and you need to rest too 'cuz of your leg."

"I know, but that means I would have to go home."

Kimmy thought that over a minute. "But I could call you on the phone if I had a problem."

"You could."

Doug leaned over and pointed to the bedside button. "Or you can press this and the nurse will talk to you or send someone to help you."

She eyed the button. "They will?" She studied it again. "Then I can stay here and you can go home, Mom. Okay?"

"Are you sure?" Roseanne reached past her outstretched leg and touched Kimmy's hand.

She nodded. "I'm sure. I'm seven and I'll be eight in a couple of months."

Doug lifted his brows. "I think it's more like four months."

"But I'm big now."

"You are, Kimmy. You're my big girl." Rose-anne dropped back into the chair, her leg causing a grimace as she shifted.

"I think we should get going then. What do you say, Kimmy? It's almost bedtime."

"Okay. And maybe I'll get a snack and some more ice cream. That's what the nurse said."

Nina rounded the bed to the other side. "Then it must be true."

Kimmy opened her arms to Nina, and they hugged. Before she pulled away, Nina kissed her cheek. "Sleep well, sweetie, and we'll see you to-morrow."

"Tomorrow, and maybe I'll be better."

Roseanne opened her mouth, and then closed it, and Doug was relieved. It made no sense to concern Kimmy with possibilities until tests re-vealed the truth. Then they would all know. He gave Kimmy a big hug and he and Nina walked into the corridor to wait for Roseanne to say her goodbyes.

When they were out of earshot, he drew closer to Nina. "Everything is still hanging, but hope-fully tomorrow the tests will give us good infor-mation, and I'm praying Kimmy will go home. This trek is too hard for Roseanne each day, and I know she'll want to be here all the time."

"Can't blame her, though." She eyed him. "You'd be the same kind of dad."

"Look who's talking? I can picture you having to be torn from the room if Kimmy was your child."

She eyed him a moment before a faint grin removed her serious expression. "You're right. I guess parents are often softies."

"Parents like you, definitely."

As the words left, he wished he'd been quiet, but instead of the usual frown or icy silence, for some reason, Nina's lips curved to a tiny grin. Something had made a difference. He hoped it had something to do with him.

Nina looked for Doug's car when she drove down Lilac Circle, but unless it was in the garage, he wasn't home. Still at work or Roseanne's or the hospital. She pulled into her driveway and entered through the back door.

Doug never called her home phone and he hadn't called her cell phone so she remained ignorant. Agitated by being unaware of Kimmy's diagnosis, she dropped her purse on a kitchen chair and eyed her home phone just in case. No blink to alert her to a message, so she dragged herself in her bedroom and slipped into a pair of pants and a sweater. At least she could be comfortable.

But comfort wasn't the answer. Though she longed to call Doug, she trusted him to call as soon as he knew anything. She brewed a mocha latte and wandered into the living room. After she set her mug down, she strode across the room and opened the door to check her mailbox. A couple of bills, two women's clothing catalogs and some advertisements. As she closed the door, Doug's car rolled down the street and stopped in front of her house. She tossed the mail on the nearest table and flung open the door. On the porch, the cold pierced her to the bone, but she waited for Doug to come up the walk. "What's happened? Good news or bad?"

"Both." He slipped his arm around her and steered her inside. "You'll be sick if you stand outside without a coat." His cold hand slipped into hers. "Let's sit. I need to let my head clear."

She sank onto the corner of the sofa, and he dropped into the closest chair.

"The bad part is Kimmy is contagious. It means washing her hands and our hands thoroughly. It's not likely we would catch it, and if we did, it would be a mild case probably without symptoms, but why take a chance."

Nina agreed. "And what's Kimmy's treatment?"

"Rest, lots of fluids and over-the-counter medication to reduce her fever."

Her concern remained. "Can Roseanne handle this?"

"She wants to try, but it's not wise. In her situation, she's likely to be more susceptible to the virus, and, naturally, using crutches and trying to take care of Kimmy doesn't make sense, either. But you know Roseanne. She's determined."

"And there's nothing you can do." She stopped her eye roll, but she'd noticed the attribute in his sister.

Doug tilted his head with a shake. "Time will prove us or Roseanne wrong. She's strong willed, and she'll have to be the one to admit she can't handle it. Or maybe she can."

"No matter, Doug, it's out of your hands or mine. We can pray everything works for the best."

"You're right."

She looked at him for the first time without focusing on Kimmy. He looked exhausted and cold. "You need something warm in your body. Coffee, tea, soup?"

He chuckled. "Chicken noodle for my health?"

"Whatever it takes. You looked chilled inside."

He nodded and rested his back against the chair. "Stress takes its toll. Kimmy's happy to be home, but rest is vital to her getting well quickly. I worry about Roseanne transporting glasses of water or juice to her. Unless she gets off those crutches, it's near to impossible. And I'm concerned about her healing, too. She's not supposed to put any weight on her legs yet, and I can see her doing anything to meet Kimmy's needs."

"Give her a day or two. That's all you can do." She rose. "I'll bring you something warm to drink." She left him resting against the chair back, and in the kitchen, she spotted a container of hot chocolate mix. She spooned powder into a mug and poured the hot water from her coffee-maker into it. The chocolate scent filled the air.

The aroma took her back to Christmas morning when she was a child. Her daddy would make pancakes, sausage and hot chocolate for breakfast after they'd opened her gifts from Santa. The memory warmed her even more after talking with her mother. All those wrinkles of bad memories had been smoothed, and they lay sweeter on her mind.

She carried in the cocoa and Doug accepted it with a smile. "Now, this is a treat." He took a sip and studied her. "You've become so much a part of my life, Nina, I have no idea how I lived all those years without you. Loneliness grows on a person I guess, and it's easier to withdraw even more than step out into the world. I suppose that's what I did. I concentrated on my family's needs and forgot that I might have a few of my own. I didn't see them. Now since you turned on the light, I can't live in the darkness anymore."

"You brightened my life, too, Doug. And my darkness was worse because I didn't even have the Lord to talk with or share my burdens. I lugged it all myself, thinking that I could carry the load. You and I know it's impossible. We might drag the baggage alone but it's difficult and miserable. It's self-defining. And I don't like that self anymore."

He rose from the chair and settled beside her. "I hate to bring this up, but I believe it's important to you. You're still carrying some baggage, Nina."

His look touched her heart and his meaning was clear. "I have been thinking, Doug. More than thinking. I've been doing some research, and I don't want to get my hopes up, but I'm closer to action than I've ever been."

His tender look melted her heart. He took the mug from her hand, set it on the nearby table and drew her into his arms. His eyes captured hers, and as he lowered his lips, the sweetness flowed through her body. His kiss strengthened and she yielded to it and a depth of love she'd never experienced. They had shared more in their months together than Todd had been willing to give—honesty, tenderness, joy and even heartbreaks—each the rhythms of life.

Doug eased back, his breath quick. "Nina, you've become an amazing part of my life. I'm so thankful that you're willing to think about seeing a physician. I promise you, I care about you without promise of children, but I believe you deserve a chance to know the truth. If another doctor agrees with the first diagnosis, I will never ask again, but you are entitled to another chance."

She lifted her hands to his cheeks, studied his eyes filled with assurance and touched his lips with hers. He drew her closer, blending their hearts as one with every beat. She trusted him. She believed in him. She longed to learn the truth.

On Friday, Doug arrived home with Kimmy and settled her into her old bedroom. Though it had taken three days, Roseanne finally admitted caring for Kimmy's needs was more than she could handle.

Kimmy had showed no qualms when he picked her up that morning. She'd kissed her mother's cheek and listed a set of rules for her mother's well-being. Doug had to control his laughter while Kimmy gave her orders with such authority.

Roseanne hugged him goodbye, and he promised to bring her home for a visit. As soon as she could get around without the crutches, Kimmy would return home for good this time. Her doctor had given Roseanne hope that it could happen soon.

Since Nina had gone to work that morning, he wanted to surprise her. He'd been tempted to call her but had resisted. Instead, he kept his eye on her house, hoping he'd notice when she arrived home from the office, which was often halfway through the day.

Though Kimmy's headache had eased with medication, she still needed rest. After gazing down the block one more time, he filled a container with apple juice, snapped on the lid and carried it to her room.

Her eyes were closed, so he tiptoed in and set the juice on the nightstand before creeping toward the doorway.

"Where's Nina?"

Surprised, he turned toward her and moved to her bedside. "She's at work, but she'll be home soon and I'll call her." He lifted the plastic tumbler and slid in a straw. "Can you sit up and drink some juice? It's apple."

She didn't move for a moment, and then eased herself up on the pillow and took a sip of the drink. "When will I be better, Uncle Doug?"

A serious expression played on her face, and his lungs pressed against his breastbone. "We'll see in another week. You should have more energy and be able to do a few things, but rest and fluids will get rid of the virus. When your symptoms are better, then we'll know you're on your way to recovery."

"It's going to be Christmas and I'll miss it." Her eyes rimmed with moisture.

He sank to the edge of her bed and slipped his arm around her. "You won't miss Christmas. You'll be better before that, I promise." He lifted a prayer that his promise didn't disappoint her. He could only guess from the physician's prognosis.

She took another sip, a larger one this time, and handed him the juice.

He set the container back on the stand and tucked her in before heading back to the window.

When he looked outside, he spotted Nina's car in the driveway. His pulse skipped as he pulled out his cell phone and hit her number. When he heard her voice, he managed to monitor his excitement. "I see you're home."

"What? Aren't you at work?"

"I had extra vacation days for working on that long project so I decided to take the day and give Roseanne a hand."

"Doug, you're the best brother there is. That's not much of a vacation for you."

He grinned to himself, hanging on to the surprise with a death grip. "When you get a chance, come down. I want to show you something."

"What?"

"Come down and see."

She chuckled. "You must have bought yourself a Christmas gift. I'm changing my clothes and I'll be down soon."

He disconnected and paced, as time ticked past. He'd become as excited as a child waiting for Christmas, but a guilty one. Though he felt bad for Roseanne, his selfish side arose again. Despite his guilt, he knew it really was best.

Though he'd doubted his every step with Kimmy until Nina came along, now he realized that if he had been that bad, he wouldn't be so eager to have Kimmy back. Maybe he hadn't done such a bad job. He'd missed the joy of having someone in his life that he had to stay one step ahead of.

Her giggles and excitement had wrapped around his heart. Another person to share his days, his hours. Nina fell in line with those changes, too. She'd slipped into the lonely niche in his heart and filled it with new life and new hope.

A knock jarred him from his thoughts and he hurried to the door to open it before she rang the bell. He hoped Kimmy wouldn't hear her arrive until she had rested.

When he swung open the door, she arched an eyebrow. "I'm curious, you know." She stepped inside. "I've never heard you so excited. I know you bought something new."

"Wrong. Nothing new and it was free."

A frown dashed across her face for a fleeting minute and ended when Kimmy's voice sailed into the room.

"Is Nina here?"

Her eyes widened, and she sped past him and vanished into the guest room. Their voices merged, both talking at one time. He stayed away for a moment to give them time, and then sauntered in to be part of the new situation.

When he came through the doorway, Nina looked at him with a grin. "We have our girl awhile longer."

"Am I your girl?" Kimmy's tired face brightened with a grin. "My mom can't carry my food and drinks even though she tried." A faint titter left her. "She tried to put a tray around her neck and it tipped over and everything spilled on the floor." She looked at them with a shrug. "I knew it wouldn't work, but she thought it would."

Doug strode across the room. "That shows you how much she wanted to have you with her."

"But I want Mom to get better. She would hurt her bones trying to do everything, and I like staying here. I told her I would come to visit when I felt better."

"Once you're rid of the headache and all the stiffness, and your fever's totally gone, then you can visit and even go back home."

She nodded with a look that said she had figured that out by herself.

Kimmy's gaze shifted to Nina. "Can we make ornaments while I'm here?"

Nina brushed her cheek. "As soon as you get rid of that fever, we will make them. How does that sound?"

"Good." She lowered her head to the pillow, wearing a content expression.

They stayed beside the bed until her eyelids drooped. Doug eased from the room, and Nina soon followed. "I know this is for the best, but I can't help but feel sorry for Roseanne's situation. She had been so hopeful."

Doug drew closer. "I don't think it will be that long, and meanwhile, she'll enjoy getting ready for Christmas here, and then I'll have to help her mom do something to make the house look like Christmas."

"We can help Roseanne."

He caught her meaning and drew her into his arms. "We can. I don't think I can manage without you."

She gave him a playful poke but her eyes said more.

His heart read her message, and he lowered his lips as she honored his kiss without restraint. Though he had questioned her feelings and understood her reservations about commitment, the message had changed. In the past weeks, the assurance had grown that Nina loved him, and her willingness to consider having a second doctor's opinion validated his confidence. Trying to imagine life without Nina had grown hopeless. One day she would be his wife. Yet despite his strong belief, he lifted his eyes heavenward and asked the Lord for His blessing.

Chapter Thirteen

"Kimmy, you'd better rest awhile. Doctor's order." She grimaced but did as Doug asked.

He looked at the clock. He'd called Nina's cell phone but she hadn't answered and that concerned him. She'd be anxious to hear how the visit to Roseanne's had gone, and he'd expected her to be clinging to her phone.

Since pacing hadn't accomplished anything, he slumped into his chair and sorted through all he and Roseanne had discussed. He knew the time would come again when Kimmy returned home, and he tried to be happy for that day.

His cell rang and he hit Talk. He opened his mouth to greet Nina and then stopped short when he heard his mother's voice.

"I haven't heard anything lately, Dougie. How's Kimmy? Roseanne? I hate to call in case they're sleeping. You know I worry."

"Sorry, Mom." He'd been neglectful recently.

He wouldn't like to be neglected by his children either—if he ever had any. "They're both doing well. Kimmy should be released from the doctor's care next week. It's just about Christmas vacation at her school, so I'll just get some of her work, and she'll go back after the New Year."

"That's good news. And Roseanne?"

"Off her crutches next week, and Kimmy will go home."

"Wonderful. We need to get over that way and—"

"You're coming here for Christmas dinner, aren't you?"

"We are. It's not that far off, is it?"

Doug grinned. "No, it's right around the corner. If it's too hard to make the trip, then just come for Christmas. You can spend the night here if you'd like."

"Wonderful. Maybe we'll do that."

The conversation ran on and finally, with the promise of seeing him soon, his mother hung up.

When he wandered into the bedroom to check on Kimmy the doorbell rang. This time he had no doubt. He hurried to the door and when he opened it, Nina grinned and stepped inside. "I've been anxious to hear how things went. I thought you might call."

"I did. More than once."

"You did?" She patted her pocket. "I went to

El's and I forgot it. I'd been glued to it before I left."

He glanced behind him, making sure they were alone, and then brushed her lips with a kiss. "Kimmy's in bed for a while. I feared she would hear you and bound out here again."

She lowered her voice. "I'll be quiet. Tell me what happened."

He filled her in on Roseanne's health, and then told her what she didn't want to hear. "Since she'll be off the crutches next week naturally she wants—"

"Kimmy home."

He nodded.

"I can't blame her, Doug. I'd want the same."

"So would I. But if you want to do those pine-cone ornaments, you'll need to fit them in this week."

"I planned to, and maybe we could get your tree decorated while she's here." She thought a moment. "I'll go home and bring over what we need to make the ornaments. Then if she gets tired, she'll be home. It's easier." She tilted her head in that direction. "I have a couple things to do, and then I'll come back."

When she looked at him a moment, he saw a sparkle in her eyes. Her lips touched his with a kiss he would never forget. When she eased back, he caught his breath, but before he could say a word, she hurried out the door, leaving him with a warm and wonderful memory.

While he waited, he pictured the few ornaments he'd packed away in the garage. If he put up a tree, and it sounded as if that was Nina's plan, he would need to do an inventory. But the most important part of a tree would be buying one. He grinned at his silliness.

He pulled out a recent newspaper and looked through the ads to see where Christmas trees were sold. His thoughts drifted, and he imagined what it would be like to shop for a tree with Nina at his side and a child or two, excited about selecting the tree. No artificial trees for him. He'd grown up in a live tree home. He wanted to continue that tradition.

"Uncle Doug?"

He laid the paper on the table and rose, wondering what Kimmy wanted. She had slipped off the blankets and sat on the edge of the mattress. "What's up, sweetie?"

"Can I get up? I'm tired of being in bed, and I feel better." Wrinkles formed between her brows and her mouth bent down at the edges.

Her pleading look caused his heart to twinge. "The doctor said you still need to rest."

"If I'm tired, I promise I'll rest. I could rest on the sofa, couldn't I?"

He looked down the hall toward the living

room and guessed what had stirred her. "I suppose the sofa is as good as the bed for rest."

A grin replaced her imploring scowl. She slid on her bathrobe and slippers and hurried past him through the doorway. When she reached the living room, she came to a halt and turned to look at him. "Where's Nina?"

His suspicion had been validated. "She went home for a while."

"Home? But I thought—"

"She'll be back soon." He crossed to the sofa and patted the cushion. "You heard her."

She nodded. "But I really feel fine. I think the doctor is being too careful."

"Ah, so you have a medical degree?" He arched a brow, unable to hide his grin.

She giggled and shook her head. "But he is being careful."

"Yes, but that's because he wants you to get better without setbacks."

She ambled to the sofa, propped up the pillow and rested her head on it.

He grasped the newspaper ads and strode toward the chair when he heard a faint knock on the door. Veering his direction, he opened it and beckoned Nina inside.

She took two steps in and chuckled. "I see the patient isn't into resting."

Kimmy peeked at her through half-open eyes. "I'm better, but the doctor doesn't know it."

"Is that right? Well, maybe then we can work on something I have in this bag."

Kimmy widened her eyes and rolled on her side. "What is it?"

Nina reached into the sack and pulled out two pinecones.

"Ornaments." Kimmy's voice rattled the windows. She pulled herself upward and slipped her feet to the floor. "Can I help?" She eyed him, her pleading expression returned. "Can I, Uncle Doug?"

"For a while." He turned to Nina, sending her a subtle grin. "Is the kitchen table best?"

She nodded. "It's safer there, but you'll want to cover it with newspaper. I have glue and glitter."

She made them sound like weapons, and he laughed. He clasped the stack of papers he'd been looking through and headed for the kitchen. By the time he'd protected the table, Kimmy had arrived and anchored herself to a chair. Nina opened the bag and emptied out numerous pinecones along with a bottle of glue and containers of red, green and gold glitter. She reached in again and pulled out a spool of red velvet ribbon.

He stood back listening to Nina explain the process and almost had the urge to give it a try himself. Instead, he contained his eagerness and watched. His heart lifted, seeing Kimmy's excitement as she painted glue along the pinecone scales, filled a plastic bag with glitter and shook it until the pinecone sparkled with gold.

"Now, let this dry while we do another." Nina brushed on the tacky glue and Kimmy selected another color—this time, red. When she pulled it out, she turned to Nina. "Can I drop it into the gold, too?"

Nina told her yes and spread out the pinecones across the table to dry. After Nina had emptied the bag of pinecones, she put a lid on the glue and poured the unused glitter into the containers. "This can dry for a few hours, and then I can hot glue the top and we can add ribbons or beads for decoration and for hangers." She leaned back. "What do you think, Kimmy?"

Her eyes sparkling with life, she opened them even wider. "I love to make these, Nina. Thank you. They will be pretty on the Christmas tree." As if struck by an idea, she turned to face him. "Uncle Doug, are you going to have a Christmas tree?"

"I am, but I have to buy it."

"Can I help?" Her enthusiasm nearly knocked her from the chair.

"I don't think so this year, Kimmy. I want to get it soon, but you can help hang the pinecones."

Her disappointment eased with his offer. "Okay, but I won't have any at home."

Nina slipped Kimmy's hand in hers. "We can

divide these up and you can pick your favorite ones. How's that?"

"I love you, Nina." She opened her arms, and he swallowed, seeing tears in Nina's eyes.

"I love you, too." She leaned into Kimmy's embrace and his heart swelled.

Kimmy released Nina's neck and turned to him again. "When are you buying the tree?"

He shrugged. He'd envisioned Nina joining him, but someone had to stay behind to be with Kimmy. His enthusiasm waned, wishing he could find a solution, but none came. "I'll need someone to stay with you when I go so I'll have to work that out."

"I can stay with her." Nina's eyes captured his.

"I know, but—" He managed to keep his wish to himself. "I may take you up on that."

Kimmy was all for it, but he eased away. Maybe, he could… What?

The obvious answer was he could go alone. He hoped this would be the last time he picked out a Christmas tree alone. It was the kind of thing people did with their family, and he finally knew how much he wanted a family.

Chapter Fourteen

Snow drifted to the ground and tipped the tree limbs and evergreens as Nina left the doctor's office, unsure where things stood. He'd explained similarities in diagnosis causing miscarriages and infertility and he'd mentioned a growth. Though it had panicked her, he'd told her not to worry. She still didn't understand fully, but he sounded hopeful, with some reservations.

Maybe she should be hopeful, too, but she didn't need to hear his uncertainties. She had prayed for good news. He'd told her that good news was possible from the tests he'd scheduled for her.

Every moment of the exam and his comments brought Doug to mind. He needed to be a father. His life would be incomplete without that blessing. And though she badly wanted children, she had lived without the hope. She could handle it, but Doug? He claimed he could. Though he would try, she feared resentment would eventually destroy their relationship.

With her heart the weight of a wrecking ball, she brushed snow off her shoes and slipped into her car to head home, where Rema had volunteered to sit with Kimmy. Rema had proven a good friend to her and Doug with her willingness to care for Kimmy when they had to be in the office. The responsibility of caring for Kimmy had given Nina a taste of motherhood. Amidst the difficulties, joy permeated every moment, whether good or bad. Her love for Kimmy had grown beyond her imagination, and proved that if she became a mother, her life would bc full.

As she pulled into the driveway, her tires leaving an imprint in the deepening snow, her cell phone's ringtone sounded. She shifted to Park and pulled the phone from her bag. Doug's face smiled at her from the screen as she hit Talk. "Why am I so honored?" She smiled at the photo.

"I've arranged someone to sit with Kimmy tonight after dinner so we can pick out our trees. Does that work for you?"

The trees. She'd assumed he would buy his without her. "Who did you get?"

"Rema volunteered. She's been great, hasn't she?"

She winced. She'd been great far more than he knew. "She has, Doug.

"How's Kimmy doing?"

Caught again. "You'll never guess that I just pulled into the driveway. I had to run an errand and Rema's sitting with her."

"She is? Maybe asking her wasn't a good idea. I just talked to her a couple hours ago."

"I'll ask her again and call you if it's a problem."

He'd accepted her solution and they disconnected, but the call left her with a pile of guilt. An errand? A doctor's appointment might be called an errand, but it left her feeling dishonest.

Facing the possibility of a good or bad diagnosis burdened her, and until she knew one way or the other, she wanted to avoid a discussion. In her mind, talking about it would only create more stress and confusion. She leaned back, watching the flakes glide through the air and land on her windshield. When she could no longer see outside, she opened the door and stepped into the white carpet of cold, as icy as her spirit had become.

Lord, give me hope.

She trudged onto her porch, plastering a pleasant look on her face. Rema was too discerning. She captured the image of selecting a Christmas tree with Doug. Her heart lightened as she opened the door.

Bundled in her warmest jacket, scarf and gloves, Nina eyed the tree lot from Doug's car, the heater and seat warmer making her cozy. Outside the snow continued to drift and she glanced at her boots, hoping they were high enough to keep out the icy flakes.

He pulled into the lot and turned off the motor. "Ready?" He sent her a coy grin. "I chose a day we may be buried in a snowbank."

"Adventure is good." She stepped into the snow as the cold penetrated the leather.

Doug held out his hand, and she grasped it, following him into the rows of trees. In the dusk, the trees were lighted by strands of overhead lights reflecting off the diamond flakes resting on the branches. Douglas fir, balsam, blue spruce. They studied the trees, estimating height and structure for open spots to hang the ornaments.

Near the back of the lot, a tree caught her interest and when she slowed, Doug did the same.

"Now, that's a beauty." Doug shifted around the tree. "It's great on all sides. I can put it in the picture window with no problem."

She studied the branches, each growing smaller to the top of the tree with open spaces to hang the ornaments. "Perfect."

He gazed at her, snow landing on his lashes, and her pulse skipped.

She lifted her finger to brush away the flakes, but he captured it with a kiss that warmed her hand. "Doug, this is the best Christmas I've had in…forever."

He drew her closer, his foggy breath whispering past her. "It's mine, too, Nina."

The look in his eyes melted the ice chilling her body, and when his lips touched hers, it sent rays of sun to her heart. She yielded again to his kiss, longing for blessings to make her able to announce her love to the heavens.

The rustle of trees eased them apart as a man strode between branches. "Did you find what you were looking for?"

Their eyes met and the glow of love they'd experienced had been exactly what she was looking for.

Doug eased away and pointed to their selection. "What is this?"

"A good choice. The balsam fir is our most popular. Short needles and strong branches with spaces for different-size ornaments. It has a long life in your home and the strongest scent of any Christmas tree."

"We're convinced." Doug grinned. "We'll take this one."

The man dragged it away for them, but Doug faltered. "What about you? Did you want to pick out a tree?"

"I've thought about that, Doug, but I'm spending most of my time at your house, and I have a small artificial tree that I think will work for this year. But if you need ornaments, I have more than I need so I can share."

His questioning look faded. "If you're sure."

"Positive, and if you'd like to buy more lights or ornaments, we can make a quick stop on the way home."

"Maybe we will."

He slipped his hand into hers as they returned to the front of the lot. The overhead lights glittered in the snowdrifts like a fairyland of glitter and gleam, matching the glow of her heart.

Four days later, Doug carried the tree from the garage to the living room, set it into the tree stand and placed it in the center of the picture window. Kimmy bounced around the living room like the seven-year-old she'd been for the past months before her illness. When Kimmy had begun to recover, it bolstered everyone's holiday spirit. Kimmy's temperature was near normal, and though the doctor advised another week of rest and fluids, he'd given her permission to spend more time being active.

Doug had wrestled with his emotional attachment to her and had accepted that she would return home that evening after the tree trimming since her mother was now off her crutches. He was grateful that she could be there to help decorate and make the occasion special.

As soon as he'd strung the white lights, which had been Nina's request, Kimmy darted to her room and carried in the box filled with glittery pinecones. "Can we put the ornaments on the tree now?"

Doug shook his head. "Can we wait for Nina? She'll be here soon, and then we can all enjoy the fun."

Though she thought a moment, she agreed that they should wait for Nina.

The wait was short. Nina arrived carrying a small box just as he'd finished fetching the new ornaments he and Nina had purchased and the box of older ones he'd used in years past.

She stomped snow from her feet onto the door-mat and handed him the box. "Here's some more ornaments if you need them. I have plenty on my tree."

He accepted the box and put them beside the others while she removed her coat and hung it in the closet.

"Let's decorate." Kimmy had latched on to Nina and tugged her to the box of pinecone ornaments.

Nina gave her a hug. "Let's keep those for last so they get the best spots."

Kimmy's eyes brightened. "Okay." She gazed at the other boxes. "Which ones go on now?"

Doug shook his head and chuckled. "Let's get organized after we turn on some Christmas music and I make us some hot chocolate."

"Yummy." Kimmy skipped her way to the kitchen as Doug followed.

Nina stayed behind and soon he heard Christmas music drifting through the doorway. She appeared shortly after with a demure grin. "I love the TV station with music for the holiday season."

"Me, too." He slipped his arm around her shoulders as the teakettle whistled. He reached into the cabinet and pulled down the chocolate mix, spooned the powder into mugs and poured in the water. In moments the fragrance of chocolate filled the air, and they moved back into the living room with their drinks.

Moving around the tree to the strains of Christmas favorites, he and Nina wove gold garland through the branches, and they all selected ornaments to hang on the tree. Kimmy worked her way around the lower branches while he reached the tall ones, and Nina hung them wherever she found spaces.

When dusk turned to darkness, the tree became heavy with decorations. He snapped on the tree lights, and the room glowed as sunny as their spirits.

"Can we now?" Kimmy stood close to the tree, holding the smaller box of decorated pinecones.

Nina cozied up to her and looked into the box. "We have about twenty of them so let's put half aside for the tree at your mom's house. What do you say?"

A frown slipped to her face. "But what about your house?"

Her chest warmed. "But you made them, Kimmy."

"We made them." Without letting her respond, Kimmy counted out the ornaments in three piles but paused holding the last two. "I need one more."

"My tree is small so give Uncle Doug one more and your mom one more. That will make me very happy."

Her eyes widened. "It will?"

"It will." She drew Kimmy into her arms and gave her a bear hug.

With the decision made, the seven glittery pinecones were added to the open spots on the tree. When they were finished, Kimmy stood back and let out a piping squeal. "It's beautiful, Uncle Doug." Her eyes shifted. "And Nina's beautiful, too."

Doug moved to Nina's side and slipped his arm around her shoulders. "I agree, Kimmy. She's as pretty as the tree." Far prettier than the tree, but he wasn't sure Kimmy would understand.

On the way back from taking Kimmy home for good this time, Nina fell silent. She'd had her tests and would soon hear from the doctor so it was time to prepare Doug for the good or the bad diagnosis. She'd been hoping she'd get some speculation from the surgeon or the technicians, but they'd said nothing despite her questions. Her doctor would study the two tests and let her know the results.

Waiting unsettled her, but she prayed for patience and for her acceptance, whatever the outcome. Though Doug had been sincere in his statement that the result would not influence his feelings, she left the door open. She'd been hurt once before and she could be wounded again. This time could result in a deeper wound, since Doug had opened her heart and her mind to loving again and this love seemed deeper and stronger than her marriage had ever been.

"Are you okay?"

Doug's question jarred her thoughts. "I'm fine. It's difficult when things change."

He reached across the space and squeezed her hand. "It's not a forever goodbye. We'll see Kimmy often. But I agree that it's different now."

Tension eased when she heard his response. Naturally, he'd considered her statement a reference to Kimmy's returning to her mother's home. It was for the best.

She initiated conversation about Christmas. They were attending a small neighborhood party to celebrate the holiday, and Christmas dinner when both of their families would meet. Her mother had called and probed her with questions about her relationship with Doug. She'd finally given in and admitted her feelings. "Finally," her mother had said with a puff of relief. "And what about your infertility?"

The question had knocked the wind from her until she found her breath. "We will deal with that when it happens. Doug knows the problem, and he seems to accept the possibility. I can only trust his word, Mom, and he's never broken it in the months I've known him."

She remained silent and Nina prepared herself for a biting remark. Instead her mother surprised her. "I would agree. He comes across as a very down-to-earth, honest man. At least, there is hope that he means what he says."

Her pulse tripped, then calmed.

"We look forward to meeting Doug's parents. I'm so glad you invited us, Nina."

"Thanks, Mom. It won't be long."

The conversation ended and she clicked off and released a lengthy sigh. The idea of their families spending time together made her nervous but worrying about it got her nowhere. Her mother had made amends and they now could look beyond the past, and Doug's family was not a threat.

By the time they'd exhausted their Christmas plans, Doug had pulled into his driveway. The glimmer of lights from the large front window lifted her spirits. "The tree looks lovely, Doug, and look at the reflections on the snow outside. It's like white cotton fluffs littered with diamonds."

He sat a moment, looking through the window, and then turned to her. "It is lovely, but as I said to Kimmy earlier, Nina, you are far lovelier than diamond-littered snow or a falling star."

He leaned closer, and she turned her face to his, accepting his kiss. When he drew back, he touched her cheek. "Let's get inside before we freeze out here."

A whoosh of icy wind filled the car when he opened his door. She unhooked her seat belt and stepped outside, meeting him halfway. He grasped her arm to keep her from slipping on the frozen surface. When they entered the house, he took her coat and motioned toward the sofa. "I'll make something warm to drink. How about some mulled apple cider?"

"Sounds good." She sank into a chair facing the tree and wrapped herself in the warmth of his kiss and the cozy Christmas decor. Yet as she waited, the admission she had to make swept through her again.

Doug came into the room whistling "Jingle Bells," and she wished her heart could be as merry as the tune.

The scent of cinnamon and orange zest passed her chair as he set a mug of cider beside her. He settled nearby on the sofa, his gaze shifting from the glittering tree to her. "You've been too quiet, Nina, and I sensed the long discussion of Christmas Day was a cover-up for something that's bothering you. Are you worried about our parents being together? I think it will be fine. I—"

"No. That's not it, Doug." She pressed her lips together, knowing she'd made a mountain out of a tiny bump in the road. "I've been wanting to tell you something, but it's been difficult."

A frown struck his face. "Did you hear something? Did you see the doctor and—"

"Yes, I saw the doctor, but I have no news."

Doug patted the seat beside him on the sofa. "Sit with me, Nina."

She rose and settled beside him. "The doctor spotted a discrepancy in the first doctor's diagnosis and he scheduled me for two tests."

"When? When will—"

"Doug, I had them already, and I should know the prognosis soon, but—"

"You've gone through this alone? Without telling me? Nina, why? You know how much I care. Why wouldn't you let me support you in this? I'm the one who asked you to have a second opinion. I did it for you as much as for me. Naturally I hoped the second doctor would disagree with the original diagnosis." Doug touched her cheek and turned her face to his. "And that's what happened."

"But it's not a sure thing, Doug. The tests may prove that—"

"They may prove anything. The first doctor was right or...the first doctor was wrong. Nina,

I'm willing to take the chance so you know for sure. You've changed your life, afraid of being left again. I've promised you that I will never go anywhere without you at my side no matter what prognosis we hear. I hoped you'd understood me and believed me."

"I trust you, Doug. I do, but—"

He nestled her in his arms. "But you're afraid to hear what they say. It's natural, Nina. You don't want to get your hopes sky-high to have them nose-dive to earth again. I understand. But we can pray that whichever we learn, we can accept it and move on. Children are wonderful gifts. Most everyone wants their own flesh and blood, but Kimmy wasn't your flesh and blood and you adored her. Can't you see that no matter what, you can have children in your life?"

Tears broke through the dam. Hearing the wise words come from him, the depth of his sincerity, had broken the floodgates. He cuddled her against him until she calmed, and then he peeked at her, puckered his lips and whistled "Jingle Bells."

How could she not adore a man who could bring her to laughter in the midst of tears? She loved him.

Chapter Fifteen

On Christmas Eve, Doug had longed to talk privately with Nina but the time got away from him. She'd been busy the day before preparing the house for her parents' visit. Though they had come to Owosso close to Thanksgiving and had planned to stay home for Christmas, something had changed their minds. Now both families would be together for Christmas, and this was the perfect time for him to tell Nina how he felt about her.

But his plan failed and now they were in the midst of a neighborhood party. The only time they would have together was later tonight. The past days' tension had created concern, but when he stopped at her house to walk with her to the party, her Christmas spirit had lifted higher than Santa's sleigh. She swept into his arms, a look on her face that had been nonexistent for a long time.

Longing to understand her change, he drew in

a breath and filled two punch glasses with sparkling apple cider. As he headed back to Nina, she'd begun to talk with one of the party guests he'd never met. He didn't think Nina knew the man either, but somehow Angie knew everyone. She and Rick seemed to be the neighborhood friendship league. Though he felt guilty leaving his mother and stepfather behind, they were in good hands at Roseanne's and had encouraged him to enjoy the festivities.

As he maneuvered his way through the neighbors, El beckoned to him. Surprised to see Birdie nowhere in sight, he turned toward El, curious. "Where's your friend?"

El chuckled, the usual glint in his eyes. "Birdie'll be here soon. Her cousins invited her to their home for a visit, and she couldn't say no on Christmas Eve."

He nodded, though he was still curious about El's relationship with her. They'd become a twosome and the friendship, though unexpected by most everyone, made him happy. Companionship now meant more than Doug might have imagined a year ago. "Is your granddaughter here?"

His eyes lost their bright flicker as he gave a toss of his head. "She's over there somewhere in the corner. She didn't want to come, but I encouraged her. Finally she gave in, but I know it was against her wishes." For the first time, El had a hopeless expression.

"This is a new situation for her. Hopefully once she's here awhile, she'll change, El. We all know what to do."

"Pray. That's what I've been doing." He lowered his eyes a moment. "I've always been a proponent of prayer, and my heart aches when I face what I already know. Nothing is in my time. It's in the Lord's hands. I only wish she could find a friend. Someone closer to her age who would make her time with me more fun."

Doug's gaze drifted to the neighbor still with Nina but now with the added audience of Rema. Doug made a subtle motion toward the man. "What about him. Do you know the man?"

"Met him once. I think his name is Craig. He must have inherited his grandfather's home or maybe he's just staying there to prepare it for sale." El shrugged but continued to study the man. "I'm not sure how old he is. Hard to tell. The younger ones all look like kids to me."

Doug laughed. "I suspect he's in his mid to late twenties."

"He's only a kid then." He chortled a moment. "Once a person's close to pushing up the daisies, everyone's a kid."

"Who's a kid?"

Birdie's voice sailed between them, giving Doug the opportunity to say hello and continue to Nina with the drinks.

Nina grinned when he slipped to her side.

"Doug, this is Craig Dolinski. He lives on the turn at the end of the cul-de-sac."

"Gramps died and left the place to my dad. Since they moved to California, he offered me the house at the greatest discount I'll ever find so…you know what I did."

Doug patted his back. "Can't blame you. That was generous."

He agreed. "Mom and Dad don't need the money, and I'm just getting started."

Rema took over the conversation, and Nina eased closer, eyeing the threesome in conversation. "El looked rather serious when you were talking."

He told her El's concern, and Nina agreed with his mention of Craig. "I think I'll sidle over there and invite her to join us. What do you think?"

He agreed, and she excused herself a moment while he joined in the conversation.

Minutes passed before Nina returned with Ginger at her side. The girl's sullen look remained, but a look of interest flashed in her eyes. "You must be Ginger." Doug extended his hand. She eyed it a moment before grasping it with a less-enthusiastic shake. "I'm Doug Billings. I live across the street. I know your grandfather very well."

She gave a halfhearted flinch of her shoulders. "Gramps knows everyone, I think."

Though she seemed disapproving, her eyes

shifted to where her grandfather had settled now with Birdie. A tender look slipped to her face and thwarted her attempt to be hard and disinterested. Doug wondered what had happened to the young woman, and he prayed Ginger would heal in her own way. Without the deep frown, she was quite pretty.

Before he turned, he heard Nina introducing Rema and Craig to Ginger, and he noted that the young man's gaze connected to Ginger's for a telltale moment, and he hoped he'd been right. A friend her age might draw her back into the world again.

Ginger appeared to let down her guard and get involved in Craig and Rema's conversation. She even joined in the laughter.

When the conversation shifted to fun things to do in town, Nina gave him a poke. "I think that did the trick." She eased her head in their direction.

"We do good work."

She tucked her arm into his. "Should we stand here or be more social?"

He eyed the other neighbors around the room and suggested they meet a few more people. They worked the room, introducing themselves to neighbors they'd never formally met, and spent time with Angie and Rick, thrilled to hear a baby was on the way.

"What do you say we leave?" He monitored his

tone, not wanting to put a damper on the party if she wanted to stay. But he had too many things on his mind to stay much longer.

"I'm ready. It's been a long day."

With a quick goodbye, they slipped on their coats and stepped outside. Winter filled the air. An icy breeze whisked at his back and penetrated his limbs. He clutched Nina's arm as they made their way along the shoveled sidewalks and across the street where the tree lights brightened the windows. The hope of time alone with Nina warmed his heart. Tonight would change his life one way or the other.

As they stepped inside, warmth greeted them. He hung Nina's jacket in the closet and motioned her into the living room as he slipped his beside hers. "How about a fire?"

"It's a good night for one." She sank onto the sofa, her face hinting of preoccupation.

He let it go and added kindling and piled a fresh log on top. When the match caught the sticks, he watched it a moment. Satisfied, he settled beside her. "You seem happier than usual. Are you pleased your parents came for Christmas after all?"

"It's nice to see them, especially with the beginning of a better relationship. That's like a wonderful gift."

"I'm sure it is." He studied her face, sensing

something else distracted her. "What are they doing tonight?"

"They have some friends who live closer to East Lansing, and they decided tonight was a good time to see them. They're staying with the friends until morning. I gave them a key to the house in case I'm in church."

"That worked out well."

She nodded, a faint grin on her face. Though it had taken him a while, he suspected he had the answer to her distraction. He'd hinted at a special surprise for her at Christmas, and now he was positive she knew what it was. "Are you thinking about my surprise?"

Her lips curved upward, no longer able to hide her smile. "A little, but—"

"I knew that was it. It took a while but—"

"You're wrong."

He drew back, his pulse skipping from her abrupt response. "What do you mean?"

Her eyes captured his and a sparkle lit her face and gave her skin a rosy glow. "It's not your surprise. It's mine."

His heart skipped, constricting his lungs, and it took him a moment to speak. "Your surprise? I knew something had made you happy."

She nodded as a smile broke free.

"Tell me, Nina, before I burst. Did you hear the test results from your doct—"

"I did."

Tears swelled in her eyes but not tears of sadness. He knew they were tears of joy. "What? What did he say?"

"I have a small growth, not serious, but preventing a safe birth. A noninvasive procedure can change that, and then there's no reason I can't have a baby, the Lord willing."

He opened his arms, drawing her into his embrace, tears rimming his eyes with the same happiness he witnessed in her face. "I'm so relieved for you, Nina. I know that apprehension had overtaken your life but you're free now. Free to make decisions without the dread of disappointing another man."

He touched her cheek and eased her around to look in his eyes. "I told you before I would not let your problem stop me from wanting to spend my life with you, and I meant that."

He drew back his hand and slipped it into his pocket. "Earlier tonight, I came prepared with my surprise, before I knew about the doctor's call." He eased back, withdrawing the small blue velvet box from its hiding place. He held it in front of her and pressed it into her hand. "Nina, I'm asking you to be my wife. You are the love of my life, the air I breathe each day. You are the shining sun to me even in the cold of winter. I love your generosity, your honesty and your willingness to seek the truth. You trusted me and saw the new doctor. And you love children, Nina. I pray the Lord blesses us with children. If not, I pray we can agree to adopt a child who needs love and a home."

A sob broke from her throat, and she looked at him with a flood of tears that spoke of love. "I want to marry you more than anything else in my life, Doug. You helped me become the woman I never suspected was in me. You opened windows and doors. You taught me all the things you say you admire in me. You are everything I could ever want and more."

He opened the box, and she gazed at the diamond with clusters on each side, glinting in the light of the Christmas tree. The fire crackled and flames licked the burning log, warming the room as it warmed their spirits.

When he slipped the ring on her finger, Nina brushed his cheek and brought her hand to his neck, her lips greeting his with a new life and depth he had never known. His heart sang carols of love and peace, and a faint jingle in his chest made him smile. Tonight he had experienced the real meaning of jingle bells.

Nina's joy was heightened by the beauty of the Christmas Day worship service. Carols soared to the vaulted ceiling, the message rang with hope and peace, and her heart warmed at the sight of Doug, Roseanne, Kimmy and Doug's mother and stepfather side by side along the church pew. Another new experience Doug had given her.

Her ring glistened in the overhead lights circled with colorful glass. Wreaths and garland draped from arch to arch along the walls, and candles glowed in sconces. Today her world had opened. Fear had flown away and hope had sprung free from the depths of her being. As the service ended with the glorious carol "Joy to the World," the congregation rose and filed down the aisles, greeting one another with hugs and handshakes.

She'd attempted to keep her ring hand hidden from his parents until the announcement when they had all gathered. The scene created visions of congratulations and good wishes from his family, and she prayed from hers, as well. Still fearing an outburst from her mother, she worked to keep the anxiety at bay. If she had only learned one thing in her journey to faith, she'd learned that the Lord was in charge. She was but a reed in the wind.

A chill clung to the air, but the sun sent bright rays into the sky, which helped to dispel the gloom of winter. The news they would share later when her parents arrived would be the brightest moment of the day.

When they rolled onto Lilac Circle, her parents' car was parked in her driveway so Doug pulled in and she headed inside, promising to see them shortly. She knew that Doug's parents had already caught on that Doug and she had made a commitment to each other. Whether they knew anything else, she would learn later that day.

She hurried inside, keeping her hand covered with her coat or stuffed into a pocket. She joined them in the kitchen for coffee before suggesting they leave for Doug's.

"You went to church—is that right?" Her mother's eyes darkened with her question.

"It was beautiful, Mom." Instead of getting defensive, she shared the message, the carols and choir, and ended with the decor. "I was glad I attended."

"I suppose you were with Doug…and that little girl. What's her name?"

Nina gritted her teeth beneath her smile. "Doug and his family. Roseanne is off her crutches and doing well. Kimmy is back to normal. Their healing was a true gift to all of us."

Her mother studied her a moment. "I'm sure it was. That little Kimmy is a sweet child."

"She is, Mom. One day I hope to have a little girl of my own." She swallowed, anticipating her mother's response.

"But…what are you saying, Nina?" Her mother pinned her with a look. "Are you telling me that—"

"I am, Mom. I saw a new doctor, and after the exam, he recommended a couple of new tests." She explained the findings and the anticipated solution, and as she talked, her mother's expression grew tender.

"That's amazing news, Nina." Tears inched from beneath her lashes, and she reached across the table to grasp her hand. "Did you hear that, Howard?"

"I'm sitting here, ain't I?"

"Aren't you." Her mother gave him a frown.

"Nina, that's the best gift you could have given me. I'm not a faith-filled woman as you are, but if anyone can bless you, it's God. I know that."

Nina's eyebrows arched with the double surprise. "Thank you, Mom. I'm pleased you're happy for me."

Her mother's gentle look and nod said more than words.

"Are you ready to walk down to Doug's? It's a short walk. Just five houses down."

"I think I can do that." She rose and Howard followed her through the kitchen doorway into the living room.

Nina grabbed her coat and led them down the street to Doug's. When they entered, the smell of ham hung on the air. She'd convinced him a turkey and stuffing was too much work, and he'd finally agreed on a ham. She'd helped prepare a few things in advance and delivered them before church, and since they'd returned from the Christmas service, his mother had taken charge in the kitchen.

Introductions took a few moments, but soon her mother had donned an apron and had joined in stirring and cutting, while Nina worked to keep her hand undercover and help as much as they would let her. Kimmy and Roseanne finished setting the table, and before too much time passed, they gathered around the dining room table.

"Let's have Christmas music?" Kimmy ran from the dining room and found the TV holidays carols they had listened to before. The background music heightened the spirit, and Doug held out his hands while others joined hand in hand. Even her mother and Howard caught on to the tradition and joined in.

Doug's gaze swept around the table. "I'm so pleased to have all of you here to join in the Christmas celebration, praising the Lord for His greatest gift, His Son, our Savior who came down from heaven to bring peace, joy, hope and salvation. Heavenly Father, we thank You for this wonderful day, for the presence of our families, and we thank You for Roseanne's and Kimmy's health. We ask You to bless this food, bless those around the table, and bless Nina's and my promise of love everlasting when we become man and wife. Amen."

The amen tangled in the surprised sounds coming from everyone at the table. "Nina." Roseanne's voice reached her. "I've been praying for this. I'm so happy."

"Thank you, Roseanne, and—"

"You could add me to the list." Her mother had risen and came to her chair, her arms opened.

Nina rose as Doug had done, and received the hugs, kisses and congratulations from everyone along with the surprise they expressed. She showed her ring, and Kimmy clung to her, gawking at the ring but most of all repeating her new litany. "You're my auntie Nina. You're my auntie Nina."

"I am, Kimmy, and I'm so happy I'll be your real auntie." They hugged and laughed as the others, still amazed, settled down again to enjoy the food.

Though she put food on her plate, Nina's appetite had vanished. Instead, she was filled with gratefulness for her wonderful news, and amazed that Doug had asked her to be his wife on Christmas Eve.

As the meal ended, Doug rose and picked up something from a cabinet sitting in the dining room. He walked around the table to Nina's seat and drew her up. When she stood beside him, he drew her closer and raised his hand above her head while everyone laughed.

"It's mistletoe, Nina." She looked at Roseanne, wearing a grin.

Everyone cheered and applauded as Doug gazed into her eyes. She raised herself to meet his lips, enjoying the blessing of commitment, hope for children of her own, and two families who rejoiced with them. Never in her life had she anticipated a day like this one.

But then with the Lord, all things were possible.

* * * * *

Nina's Creamy Corn Casserole

Ingredients

½ cup butter, melted
2 eggs, beaten
1 14.5 oz box dry cornbread mix (I prefer
Krusteaz Honey Cornbread)
1 15 oz can whole kernel corn
1 15 oz can creamed corn
1 cup sour cream

Instructions

Preheat oven to 350°F and lightly grease a
9 x 9 pan.
In a medium bowl, combine butter, eggs, dry
cornbread mix, corn and sour cream.
Pour batter into baking dish.
Bake for 45 minutes or until top is golden
brown.

Dear Reader,

I hope you enjoyed *A Husband for Christmas*, book two of the Lilac Circle series, and the blend of unique characters who weave their way through this series. In Angie Bursten's story, *A Mother to Love*, you met Nina Jerome. I hope you were touched by the theme of love, a love blessed by the Lord. In their journey Nina and Doug realized their views on love and marriage had been molded by different philosophies, resulting in their fear of marriage. Nina struggled with her secret wounds from being rejected by a man who promised to love her for better or for worse. Doug's view was influenced by marriages that didn't encompass the depth that he wanted in a relationship. Instead he provided love and support for everyone but himself. Yet with prayer and awareness of the self-made barricades that warped their lives, they found that Christmas opened doors for a reminder of God's love, an amazing relationship of forgiveness and trust providing a true look at the greatest love of all. I hope you are anxious to meet the next characters in the third novel of the Lilac Circle series.

Gail Gaymer Martin

LARGER-PRINT BOOKS!

GET 2 FREE
LARGER-PRINT NOVELS
PLUS 2 FREE
MYSTERY GIFTS

Love Inspired®

Larger-print novels are now available...

LILP

LARGER-PRINT BOOKS!

GET 2 FREE
LARGER-PRINT NOVELS
PLUS 2 FREE
MYSTERY GIFTS

Love Inspired®
SUSPENSE
RIVETING INSPIRATIONAL ROMANCE

Larger-print novels are now available...

LISLP15

READERSERVICE.COM

Manage your account online!

- Review your order history
- Manage your payments
- Update your address

*We've designed the
Reader Service website
just for you.*

Enjoy all the features!

- Discover new series available to you,
  and read excerpts from any series.
- Respond to mailings and special
  monthly offers.
- Connect with favorite authors at
  the blog.
- Browse the Bonus Bucks catalog
  and online-only exculsives.
- Share your feedback.

Visit us at:
ReaderService.com